Back Home Again

The Five59 Stories, plus a few

Lynne Cantwell

hearth/myth

Table of Contents

Introduction

In 2013, several members of the BookGoodies authors group on Facebook hatched a plot to create a Halloween anthology. Alan Seeger volunteered to be our editor, Joseph Picard created the cover art, and the first-ever *13 Bites* began to come together. The idea was to include thirteen stories, but we didn't have a ton of participants back then, so some of us – including me – contributed a second story to bring us up to the magic number.

Not long after that, the anthology group hived off from BookGoodies to become its own thing. Alan set up shop as an editor and publisher – his company is called Five59 Publishing – and began to solicit submissions from us for four anthologies per year. We've tried a variety of themes and genres, but we're starting to settle into a rotation that seems comfortable for nearly everyone. Currently, *13 Bites*, which features horror stories, is released every October; *Other Realms*, our fantasy anthology, will be released each January; and *Plan 559 from Outer Space*, our annual science-fiction collection, is released each April. The fourth publication is the group's choice, and this year it's *559 Ways to Die* – detective stories, murder mysteries, and the like.

I say "we," but it's really Alan's baby, and he is awesome. He does all the hard work – editing, formatting, herding authors – while we, the contributors, get to have all the fun.

I've found participating in these anthologies to be a great way to stretch as a writer. I've written the occasional horror story over the years, but I tend to shy away from writing sci-fi and even some types of fantasy. I've been trying some new stuff as a result of this process, and sometimes the results are even decent.

Another way to stretch as a writer is by creating flash fiction. I'm on the staff at Indies Unlimited, where we host a flash fiction contest every week. It's a challenge to squeeze an entire story into 250 words; even if you don't win, you can't help but become a better writer as a result of the exercise.

The stories in this collection were all written between the fall of 2013 and the spring of 2016 – mostly for the Five59 anthologies, but

I've included a few outliers (hence the "plus a few" in the subtitle). Every story falls under the broad umbrella of speculative fiction – science fiction, fantasy, and horror – with the exception of "The Door Into Summer," which is magic realism. I have included a couple of spinoff stories from the *Pipe Woman Chronicles* universe, but most of what you'll find here has nothing to do with that series. Still, I hope you enjoy this book – and if you do, I hope you will go back where you purchased it and post a review. Pretty please? Reviews are a key way that readers find good books, and I treasure each and every review that my books receive.

Also, to get the first word on all of my new releases, please sign up for my spam-free newsletter at http://eepurl.wwx9d. The newsletter is your guaranteed way to find out what's coming up, and I only darken your inbox with them four or five times a year.

One more thing: If you're a writer who's interested in contributing to the Five59 anthologies, go to www.five59.com to contact Alan. We'd love to have you! And if you're keen to try your hand at flash fiction, it's even easier – just head on over to indiesunlimited.com any Saturday, find the contest post, and write your entry in the comment box. Hope to see you there!

Lynne Cantwell
July 2016

Distaff

It's good, I think, to have a second creative outlet, for those times when your primary one is making you crazy, or for when you've finished a big project and need to rest your brain before jumping into the next one. For me, fiber arts fill the bill. Usually I knit, but sometimes I use a drop spindle, also known as a distaff – an ancient device for making thread. A number of pagan pantheons have a god (or two or three) in charge of spinning the threads of life; perhaps the most well-known are the Greek Fates, or Moirai. They were on my mind when I wrote this dystopian sci-fi story, which appeared in Plan 559 from Outer Space Mk. II *in the spring of 2016.*

The after-lunch crowd filled the schoolyard with shouts and giggles, as it did every day. Moira pulled up the hood of her jacket and threaded her way through the throng. As usual, no one took any notice of her. Maybe the administrators did, as they stood on the stoops of the classroom building and the dormitories. Or maybe they were just getting a breath of spring air. She never looked up at them; if they were watching her, she didn't want them to know that she knew.

Silent as a monk, she shuffled past the red-brick buildings, through the red dirt of the yard, to her usual spot near the fence. It, too, was red brick, and it blocked her view of the outside world. But sometimes a blade of grass would appear along the edge – a courageous green wisp that tethered her to the life she had had before coming to this place.

As she turned to sit, her toe dislodged a rock from the dirt. It was flat and nearly circular, with a hole poked through in the middle. She sucked in a breath as she picked it up. It reminded her of grass and trees; of days in the shade with her mother and grandmother...

"What have you got there?"

Startled, Moira reflexively shoved her hand into the pocket of her hoodie. Then she looked up. "Nothing," she said.

The girl was smiling in a friendly manner. She looked to be about the same age as the oldest students at the school. "You're Moira, right? I'm Nadine." She crouched next to Moira as she stuck out her hand and waited.

Moira dropped her find in her pocket and shook hands politely. "I know. How's your first day going?"

"Oh, you know." Nadine's smile faded a bit as she glanced around the dirt schoolyard.

"I don't know, actually. I've never been to another school."

Nadine stared at her. "Really? I've never known anyone who's been able to stay in one place that long."

I lived in the same house my whole life, until the authorities came... But Moira knew better than to speak the words aloud. She slipped her hand into her pocket again and clenched her find in her fist.

Nadine watched the movement. "Can I see it?" she asked gently.

Even as Moira shook her head, she was drawing out her prize. "Just a rock," she said, shrugging, as her mother and grandmother both screamed warnings in her head. But their words were echoes, their voices long since stilled. She opened her fingers to let Nadine see.

"Cool," the new girl said. "It's got a hole in the middle. I bet if you…" Her eyes widened as her mouth snapped shut.

Moira sighed inwardly as she shoved the rock back in her pocket. "You'd better go," she said, unnecessarily. Nadine was already on her feet and backing away from her. Two more steps, and she turned and ran.

The thing was, Nadine was right. If Moira had a stick, she could fit it into the hole in the rock. Then she would have a distaff. A spindle. A thing forbidden. For a distaff could spun the planet's energy into whatever a person needed: a job, a house, a baby. Peace among neighbors or within families. Love. Life.

Moira knew how to wield a distaff. Her mother had taught her. It's what had cost her her life.

The bell rang; the lunch period was over. Moira sighed and dropped the rock. It wouldn't do to have it on her when she went back inside. One of the administrators might find it — and if they hadn't been keeping an eye on her previously, that would surely make them start.

But she marked in her head where she had dropped it, just in case she ever found a stick.

Moira daydreamed through her classes, as usual. She was an indifferent student, but it didn't matter. The students at this so-called school were never tested on anything they were supposed to be learning, nor were they ever encouraged to learn anything other than the material presented to them. The authorities paid no attention to their grades or natural aptitudes when assigning them jobs. They were all just parked here for the requisite number of years, from the ages of twelve to twenty-two, in order to learn how to be good little cogs in the authorities' machinery. You didn't need to be creative to do that. You only needed to know how to do what you were told.

Moira's mother had been no good at doing what she was told. She had insisted on being creative. *And look where it got her.*

Moira was nearly nine the day the authorities carried her mother away. It had been a beautiful summer day, sunny and warm, and the three of them — Moira, her mother, and her mother's mother — worked in the shade of the lanai. They had done so for as long as Moira could remember. Her mother had begun training her on the distaff at the age of five, and she was proud of her thin, strong energy lines that hardly ever broke. It was important that she spin strong lines, for breaking it was her grandmother's job.

Mother had just sent her into the house to refill their lemonade glasses when the big black cars drew up in front of their house. Moira watched from the window as the men approached her mother and grandmother. Voices were raised. Mother stood up and took a step toward the men, her ruler in her fist. The men restrained them both, and robbed Mother of her ruler and Grandmother of her shears. Then, when Mother stomped down on her captor's instep, he hustled her to one of the cars.

"Mama!" she cried.

Mother saw her at the window. "Remember, my daughter!" she called as the men stuffed her into their car. "Remember how to spin!"

That's when one of the men pulled his gun and shot her.

Her grandmother began to wail. The man restraining her shook her hard, and said, "Shut up, you old bag, or I'll shoot you, too!" So her grandmother shut up, and let the men take Moira's mother away. They never saw her again.

The end-of-period bell rang. The instructor – she had never learned his name – ceased his droning as the students packed their things and began shuffling off to their next class. Moira glanced at the doodles she had made in her notebook, and blanched at what she had drawn: a thin line, wound over and around itself, that threw off sparks.

She slammed the notebook shut. She needed to be more careful. Especially now that Nadine had guessed her secret.

Mother's ruler and Grandmother's shears were gone forever, but Moira had tucked her distaff into her belt when she went inside. She pleaded with Grandmother to be allowed to keep it – but no. "We must put it away," the old woman said, her mouth set in the hard line that Moira would come to know well over the next few years.

"But I need it," she had protested. "We still have to work, don't we?"

For generations, the women of her family had spun, measured, and cut the planet's energy. The troubled would come from miles around – sometimes from half a world away – to appeal to them for help. The women of her family, always working in threes – the Maiden, the Mother, and the Crone – would listen solemnly and send their petitioners away. Then they would solve the problem the way they had since time immemorial: spin, measure, snip. The results were not always exactly what the petitioner had wanted, but they were always the best outcome for everyone involved. That was the planet's genius, not theirs. But still.

Grandmother shook her head. "No one will come to us anymore," she said sadly. "We have no Mother."

"We could find a new Mother," Moira argued.

"Enough," said Grandmother, her lips pressed into that thin line again. And that was that.

Until the day several years later, when Moira went looking for something in the attic and found her distaff. It was nestled in a velvet box that had been placed between the rafters and hidden beneath a heavy trunk. She could never have moved the trunk, but her arm was thin enough to slide under it from behind.

Delighted, she forgot all about her original errand and took her prize downstairs, out into the sunlight.

Her grandmother stormed out after her. "Have you lost your mind?" she cried, snatching the distaff from Moira and breaking the shaft over her knee.

"My distaff!" Moira wailed.

Grandmother threw the broken thing into the box and shut the lid. "Do you want us both to die like your mother did?" she said in a harsh whisper. "Leave things be, child!" She picked up the box and headed into the house, but paused on the stoop. "And stop crying! Do you want the whole neighborhood to hear you?"

Moira nursed her anger until her grandmother was back inside. Then she ran down to the creek, where she could scream her frustration without prying neighbors to hear her.

But someone must have heard something, because when she returned home late that afternoon, the men in their black cars were there. They told her Grandmother was gone and wouldn't be back, so she had to go to school. They refused to answer any questions and gave her ten minutes to pack her things. Bewildered, she threw her pajamas, her favorite t-shirt, and her teddy bear into a backpack as one of the men stood watch. Then she, too, was whisked away.

It was twilight when she arrived at the school. It seemed a forbidding place, with its sealed windows and tall fence. The evening attendant confiscated her backpack; she never saw it again. Instead, she was given a uniform – the same clothing all the other girls wore, she learned the next day – and a bed in a room with five other girls. No one spoke to her, but none of them spoke to one another, either.

And so her "schooling" began – in airless classrooms and a fenced lot devoid of any plant life. In the four years since her arrival, Nadine was the first person to offer her a word in friendship. And then she'd run away.

Sometimes Moira would puzzle over the authorities' fear of her family. She dreamed up many theories, but could not come up with a satisfactory explanation. What threat had they been? All they had done was help people solve their problems.

The answer finally came to her in the unlikeliest of places: history class. Moira was old enough to know that the new regime had rewritten the curriculum; in particular, much of the history she was being taught placed the powers-that-be in a benign light, while describing as dangerous the freedom she and her family had once enjoyed.

On this day, her attention was caught when her instructor uttered the word *fate*. Intrigued for the first time in four years, she sat up and paid attention.

"Fate," the instructor said now, "was once something individuals fought against. Instead of accepting their lot in life, people thought it proper to strive for something better. There was even a cottage industry of people – mostly women – who claimed to have magical powers in this regard."

We did, Moira thought. She had never realized there were other families like hers – but of course, there must have been. No one family could have helped everyone in the world.

The instructor droned on. "Of course, once our scientists learned how to determine the best possible life path for all our citizens, the government could not allow these charlatans to continue practicing. So four years ago, Operation Distaff was launched to root them out. Some were retrained, but most had to be eradicated."

Moira dropped her eyes to her notebook and willed herself not to cry. *Eradicated! Is that what you call it when your mother is shot dead in front of you?*

She realized with a pang that she had been nurturing a hope that her grandmother had survived. But the authorities wouldn't have bothered trying to "retrain" her; she was too old.

Moira herself, on the other hand…

She clutched her pen so hard that it snapped, drawing looks from the students around her. Blue ink covered her right hand and soaked into the pages of her notebook.

The instructor never missed a beat.

She slid out of her seat and left for the restroom, dropping her broken pen in the trash can by the door on her way out.

Once in the restroom, she washed away as much of the ink as she could. As she scrubbed, she realized why her family had been targeted: the powers-that-be didn't want any anyone to have a way to change their lives. They wanted people to accept the fate the government gave them, without complaint. She, her mother, and her grandmother had been a threat to the regime.

She would still be a threat, if she could get her hands on a distaff.

The passing bell rang. She dried her hands and began to go back to class to collect her notebook. But there was no need, for Nadine stood just outside the bathroom door with Moira's notebook in her hands.

"Thank you," said Moira, and began to walk away. But Nadine touched her forearm. The feeling of another's fingers on her skin startled her; it had been a long time since anyone had touched her.

As Moira stood still, Nadine leaned in and whispered in her ear, "I have a ruler."

We could find a new Mother… Her own words came back to haunt her. "I have no stick," she hissed back. "And we need shears."

"I know. I'll keep looking." Nadine dropped her eyes and stepped back.

Moira's thoughts were in turmoil. "Thanks again," she managed in a normal tone, and hastened away.

Moira lay awake far into the night. Questions plagued her: Would any distaff do? Did the ruler have to be a special length? Did the three women have to be related?

Was there magic to what she and her family had done? Or was it a natural talent, passed down from generation to generation, as her mother had told her?

Could they change fate?

There was no way to know without trying it, and there was no way to try. She had a weight for her distaff – assuming the rock was still where she had left it – but no stick. And they had no shears. Nor did they have a third person to wield them. And even if they had all of that, they had no private place to experiment.

The barriers seemed insurmountable.

But that's what the authorities wanted them to believe.

She rolled over and stared at the tiny table that stood between her bed and that of the next girl's. Her notebook and new pen sat on the edge. She had practically had to beg Requisitions for the pen. The lady behind the desk had seemed highly reluctant to give it to her.

At the time, it had seemed to be just one more annoyance in a series of annoyances she had come to associate with this school. But now, she wondered why.

She looked again at the pen – how straight, and round, and long it was. How the point was shaped just so.

She couldn't ask for another from Requisitions – not this soon. But if only she hadn't thrown the remnants of her old pen away.

Then she remembered how full the trash can had been. *They must not change the trash every day. My old pen might still be there.*

The thought both excited and frightened her. Sometimes there were random checks of the student quarters, often when the students were in class. If she was found to have a broken pen in her possession, things might go badly for her. At the very least, she would face some questions about why she had kept it.

But the lecture of the day before had lit a fire in her – a fire damped the day she lost her grandmother. She needed a distaff in her hands again.

As silently as she could, she slid out of bed. The school didn't bother with heat in the dormitory rooms overnight, and the concrete floor seemed to freeze her bare feet. She rubbed her upper arms briskly, then grabbed her hoodie and slipped it on for warmth before letting herself out into the hallway.

This much wasn't unusual; some girls got up in the middle of the night to use the restroom down the hall. But she would have to leave the dormitory and cross the schoolyard, and she had no idea what would happen if she tried it. Would motion-sensor lights come on? Were the grounds patrolled at night?

She was about to find out. She pushed against the front door release bar and eased her way out. A loose brick sat on the concrete porch; she knew it was sometimes used to prop the door open when it was warm out. She wedged it between the door and the jamb, in case the door locked from the inside when shut.

Then she turned and surveyed the deserted schoolyard.

The school consisted of five unconnected buildings. The two dormitories sat side by side, across the yard from the classroom building and the cafeteria. At the far end was the fifth building, which the teachers and administrators called the physical plant. The basement windows of this building cast a thin light across the yard.

The ground was even colder under her feet than the dormitory floor had been. The quickest path to the school building was a diagonal across the yard, but despite the cold, Moira decided to stick to the shadows. She dashed from her building to the front of the second dorm and waited, her heart pounding in her throat. When a few minutes had gone by with no alarm apparent, she bent over and ran to the side of the physical plant.

Now she could hear voices. Women's voices. She crept to an open window from which steam was billowing and basked in the warmth. She wished she could sit down and put her feet in the window to warm them up, too – they were beginning to feel like blocks of ice – but she didn't dare.

As she turned to go, she heard one of the women call out to another: "Sophie, hand me the ladle, would you?"

Moira froze. Her grandmother's name had been Sophie. Instead of leaving, as all of her instincts screamed at her to do, she knelt by the open window and peered in.

The steam-filled room reeked of bleach. Several women stirred things in huge copper cauldrons. One woman lifted a paddle with a fold of white cloth draped over it. *Of course! The laundry!* Someone must wash the sheets and towels, and the students' uniforms. These women must be the ones who did it.

Another woman had her hand on a huge ladle that hung on the wall. The woman lifted down the ladle and turned – and Moira stifled a gasp, for this Sophie was indeed her grandmother.

She was certain she had been quiet, but somehow Grandmother must have heard her, for she looked toward the window. Such a look of surprise and relief passed over her features that Moira nearly called her name. But then, hurriedly, Grandmother turned away from her and handed the ladle to another woman nearby. She did not look Moira's way again.

Nearly in tears, Moira backed away from the window. Her grandmother, here? How long had she been working in the laundry? Did she even know Moira went to this school? And why didn't she give her a hint of recognition, other than that fleeting look on her face?

Her mind reeled with those questions, and more besides. But there was no answer for them now, and anyway she had come out here for a reason. So she stumbled away toward the school building.

And found the door locked.

Crestfallen, she turned back the way she had come. When she reached the physical plant, she glanced at the laundry room window; light still glowed from within, but the window had been shut.

With a heart as cold as her feet, Moira made her way back to her own dormitory, slipped the brick out of the doorway, and went back to bed. No one stopped her – and it was good no one did, for they certainly would have remarked on the tears that tracked silently down her cheeks.

Any hope that she had gotten off scot-free was dashed the next morning, when the dormitory matron pulled her aside as she left for the cafeteria. They entered the matron's office – a room as Spartan as every other in the school – and sat Moira down across from her, a massive desk between them.

"Why were you out of bed last night?" the matron demanded.

Moira swallowed. "I had to pee."

"Then why did you not use the restroom? Why did you leave the dormitory instead?"

"I was confused," she said.

The matron fixed her with a gimlet eye. "What were you after in the school building?"

Moira gazed impassively at her.

The matron sighed. "Won't tell me, eh? And here we thought you had adjusted." She leaned both forearms on the desk. "Tonight, before bed, and every night for the next two weeks, you will be provided with a special tonic. You will find it on your bedside table, in a bottle marked with your name. You must drink it all, every night. I will personally check the bottle every morning to make sure it is empty. Is that clear?"

"Are you drugging me?" Moira asked, her chin up.

The matron's brow lowered. "I said, is that clear?"

Moira dropped her eyes to her lap. "Yes, ma'am."

The matron sighed again. "Go now, or you'll miss breakfast."

"Yes, ma'am," Moira said again, and scuttled out of the office.

The trash can in her history classroom had been emptied overnight.

Moira dragged through her day as if a fire had never been lit in her belly. She even forgot about the "special tonic" until she was getting ready for bed. There it sat, in a red bottle with a rubber stopper. Her name was inked plainly on the label.

"Don't drink it," the girl in the next bed over said.

Moira blinked. None of her four roommates had ever spoken, in all the years she had lived here. "What?" she blurted.

"Don't drink the tonic," the girl said again. "Oh. I'm Maddie."

"Moira," Moira managed.

"I know," said Maddie.

"We all know," said another girl. "We all know why you're here. I'm Claire."

"I'm Desiree," said another.

"And I'm Juana," the fifth girl said. "Hi."

"Hi," Moira said. "Um…why haven't any of you spoken to me before now?"

"Because you seemed so numb," Juana said. "We thought they'd already gotten to you."

"Reprogrammed you," Desiree said.

"But then we saw the bottle," Claire said. "And Nadine said…"

"How do you know Nadine?" asked Moira, feeling suddenly exposed. "What did she say?"

"Hang on and I'll tell you," Claire giggled. She was a willowy blonde with a deep tan. "I have some classes with Nadine. I saw her hand you your notebook yesterday, so I asked her how you two knew each other."

"What did she tell you?"

"Don't look so scared," Desiree said, her white nightgown making her skin look even darker than its natural coffee color. "Look, we're all in here for something the government doesn't like. I used to build rockets with my brother. We figured out how to send stuff into orbit." Her face fell. "He's dead now. The government killed him right in front of me."

"They shot my mother right in front of me," Moira said.

"My sister had an untimely accident with a surfboard," Claire said, her tone bitter. "Surfing is not an approved sport. It's too freeing to the soul, or something."

"That's what they said about music," Maddie said, her red curls bouncing as she nodded. "My father died defending his fiddle."

"My grandmother died for making art," said Juana, flipping her long, brown hair over her shoulder.

"My grandmother's here," Moira blurted.

"What?" Claire said. "Where?"

"In the laundry room," Moira said, and recounted her adventure of the previous night.

Desiree whistled low. "No wonder they gave you the tonic."

Moira eyed the bottle nervously. "What happens when you drink it?"

"Depends," said Juana. "Either you go numb, or you go crazy. The girl who had your bed before you went crazy. After three nights of the stuff, she just started screaming and wouldn't stop, so they took her away."

"Where'd she go?" Moira asked.

Juana shrugged. "No idea. She was just gone."

Moira's stomach clenched. "But I have to take it," she said. "Matron will check the bottle in the morning, and there's nowhere to pour it out."

"Ah, but there is," said Maddie, pointing to a crevice between the baseboard and the wall beside Moira's bed.

Moira looked around at the other girls. "You won't tell Matron on me?"

"And get tonic of our own?" Desiree laughed. "No, we're all in this together. Right, girls?" Heads nodded solemnly as Desiree went on, "But you have to act like you're taking it. So no more walks after hours, okay?"

"What were you after, anyway?" asked Claire.

"A broken pen that I threw in the trash in history class."

"For what?" Juana asked.

"A distaff," Moira admitted, her voice low. "I found a rock outside that would work for the whorl, but I need a stick, too." She shrugged and sagged onto her bed. "It wouldn't have worked, anyway. I would have had to figure out a way to hold the broken pieces together."

The other girls exchanged a look. Then Maddie pulled her own hoodie off the bedpost and rifled through the pocket. "Here," she said at last, handing Moira a pen. "I have a spare."

Moira's eyes stung as she took the gift. "Why are you all being so nice to me?" she asked.

"Isn't it obvious?" Desiree asked. "We want you to change *our* fates, too."

During the next day's lunch period, Moira crouched in her usual part of the schoolyard, trying to look as if she were in a daze. Her rock was already in her hoodie pocket; by some miracle, it had been just where she had left it.

There's no such thing as miracles. Or magic. Only science, according to the government. She snorted softly, keeping her face blank. *A lot they know.*

Nadine dropped to a cross-legged seat three or four feet away. "I hear you have a stick," she said softly, without looking at Moira.

"You probably shouldn't be seen near me," Moira said.

"I don't care anymore," Nadine said, her voice still low. She used a forefinger to draw random patterns in the dirt. "You've got a stick and a stone, and I've got a ruler and shears."

"You do?" Moira glanced at her, then pointedly looked away.

"Yeah. And I hear you know where we can find a Crone."

"I might. But I don't know how to reach her." Tears pricked the backs of her eyelids.

"I might," Nadine said. Her dirt doodles had begun to take on the unmistakable shape of the schoolyard. "Meet me here after supper," she said, making a lazy circle around a spot between the dormitories. "The laundry ladies have rooms in our building."

"All right," said Moira, as Nadine continued doodling, obliterating her map. The next time Moira chanced to look at her, the doodles were smoothed away and Nadine was gone.

Moira gave it another minute or two, then got to her feet slowly and made her way back to the school building. The endless afternoon before her promised to be torture. She couldn't wait for it to be over, and couldn't show it in any way.

Dusk was falling as she left the cafeteria building; she lagged behind the rest of the students, staring at her shoes as she walked, and hoped no one noticed her turn between the dormitories instead of entering her own.

The narrow strip of dirt between the buildings was already so dark that she nearly ran into Nadine. Unobserved at last, they hugged in excitement. "See there?" Nadine said, pointing to a side entrance. "That's the door to the laundry ladies' rooms. They'll be out in a minute or two, so they can head over to the physical plant."

"How do you know that?"

"My room is on the other side of the building. I see them through my window every night." Nadine leaned against the wall opposite the doorway and slid to a seat. "Might as well make ourselves comfortable."

Moira nodded and sat, but was up on her feet again a few minutes later. Nadine laughed at her. "You look like a jack-in-the-box," she said. "Come and sit by me."

But just then the door opened and five women made their way out. The last one to emerge was Sophie.

Nadine was on her feet instantly and threw an arm out to block Moira from running to her. "Let me handle this," she whispered. "We don't know what mental state she's in." Nadine then stepped into the women's path and said, "Sophie?"

"I'm Sophie," Moira's grandmother said. "Who are you?"

"I need to speak with you urgently," Nadine said. "I have a message for you."

From the shadows, Moira saw Grandmother's eyes light up, even as her mouth stayed stern. "Go on," she told the other women. "I need to see about this foolishness. I'll catch up."

The other women nodded and headed off. When they had turned the corner, Grandmother turned to Nadine. "Where's Moira? Have you seen her?"

"I'm right here," said Moira, stepping up to her grandmother at last.

Before the reunion got too soppy, Nadine intervened. "Sophie, we have more news for you."

Moira brushed away her tears and grinned. "I have a stick," she said. "And a whorl."

"And I have a ruler and shears," Nadine said.

The color drained from Grandmother's face. "Haven't you learned anything?" she said. "You'll get us all killed."

"No, Grandmother," Moira insisted. "We'll get us all freed. Everyone here is being held for doing something natural. Something beautiful. We need to help them, the way we used to."

Grandmother turned to Nadine. "You propose to be the Mother," she said.

"I *am* a Mother," she said. "My daughter was taken from me, just as yours was from you. Arienne was only..." She swallowed and began again. "She was only four. I hadn't yet begun to teach her the distaff."

Grandmother shuddered. "What they're doing isn't right."

"No, it's not," Nadine said. "And we can stop it."

"Please, Grandmother," Moira said, knowing she was wheedling.

Grandmother thought for just a moment. Then she said, "Hand me the shears."

And right there, in the shadows between the dormitories, the three women began.

Moira put the tip of her pen through the hole in the rock. Then, drawing on the planet's vast energy reserves as she had been taught, she began to spin her distaff. The energies had not been tapped by anyone in a long time; they sprang swiftly to Moira's makeshift tool and filled it in seconds. The spun energy looked so beautiful, Moira thought, all rainbow-colored and sparkling. She pulled it from her distaff and handed it to Nadine, then began spinning again.

Nadine murmured to herself as she measured the lengths and handed them to Moira's grandmother. She, too, murmured to herself as she wielded her scissors: "For Moira…for Nadine…for me. For Flora. For Angie. For Bea. For Dotty." She looked at her granddaughter.

"For Maddie. For Juana. For Desiree. For Claire." She looked straight at Grandmother, still spinning. "For Mama."

Grandmother nodded as Nadine began. "For Arienne. For Shawna…"

As more and more lengths of energy were cut, Moira became aware of a roaring noise. It was coming from inside the dormitories on either side of them. And it was getting louder.

"For Edna," said Grandmother, her shears working faster and faster. "For Isabelle. For Diane. For Naomi. For…"

"What is the meaning of this?" Matron roared as she rounded the corner and charged down the narrow corridor. "Stop this at once!"

"For Matron," Moira cried.

"For Matron," said Grandmother, and cut. Matron stopped dead in her tracks – and for the first time that Moira could remember, the woman began to smile.

"Freedom for all the people everywhere!" Grandmother said as she made her final cut.

In the wider world, no one knew what brought that terrible government to its knees. To most observers, it seemed to collapse from within.

But Moira and her grandmother knew. So did Nadine and her daughter Arienne, whom Nadine found at a school nearby. All four women moved to a little house in the woods, far from the government's prying eyes – but not so far away that those who needed help couldn't find them.

As Grandmother aged, she began to train Nadine to wield the shears; Nadine then taught Moira how to measure, and Moira in turn taught Arienne how to spin. Nadine bought Arienne her own distaff, and Moira commissioned a beautiful new distaff for herself. But she never got rid of the makeshift stick-and-stone distaff that had brought so many to freedom.

Tanaquil

Like most fantasy writers, I came to the genre by way of epic fantasy. While I've read my share, it has been a long time since I've written any myself. So for Other Realms, *the Five59 anthology published in the summer of 2015, I decided to give it a try. Here's the result.*

The longer Grand Vizier Sihlirian viewed the steaming entrails laid out upon his marble table, the tighter his features knotted. With a curt wave of his hand, the table upended itself, dumping the offal onto the exquisitely-patterned Cartagelian rug beneath.

For months, his divinations had shown him the same thing: his days as the power behind the Nantulian throne were numbered – and that number was getting smaller all the time. For thirty-five years, he had enjoyed unprecedented wealth and power, first as regent to young king Karolnu after his parents' untimely deaths (Sihlirian had not *caused* their deaths, to be clear, but he knew how to seize a golden opportunity when one presented itself), and then as Karolnu's most trusted adviser. It had been a perfect setup: his political acumen (assisted by the dark arts when necessary) and Karolnu's naïveté had brought Nantulia territory around the world and riches beyond imagining. A single attack by the Nantulian military would cause foreign heads of state to gratefully accede to Nantulian acquisition of their demesnes in exchange for keeping those heads on their shoulders.

Sihlirian had always thought negotiation was for the weak. One did not sit down for tea and talks with a lesser power; one simply took. He viewed any other course of action a waste of time.

Still frowning, he moved to the arrow-slit window of his turret workroom. Often, the sight of so much land under his control was enough to mellow his mood. But not this time. This time, the entrails had been clear: the change was at hand. And he could not prevent it. For no matter how he phrased the question – no matter how many spells he cast, no matter how many animals he slaughtered – he could not tell from which quarter the threat came.

He could not remember exactly when this weakness had begun to overcome his art; every time he considered the question, his thoughts uncharacteristically skittered away. But from what he could recall, it might have begun on or about the time of Karolnu's final campaign. Or before that. Or perhaps afterward. He simply could not recall – and the effort gave him a headache.

As he massaged his forehead, he turned from the window and surveyed its appointments: the priceless tapestries upon the walls, the chairs covered in raarbiist leather from outer Langellia, the flasks and beakers of mouth-blown Totol crystal that he used in his work. The scrolls looted from the world's finest libraries. The tiny drawers crammed full of the most exotic herbs and other nameless substances he used in his sorcerous activities. His own rich apparel, from the jeweled cloak pin at his shoulder to his dyed raarbiist boots.

All a testament to a comfortable life. An almost-perfect life.

What a time for his art to fail him!

With a roar of frustration, he threw his hands toward the entrails whose unwholesome fluids were soaking into the rug. The traitorous offal disappeared in a giant ball of green flame, leaving not even a damp spot behind.

Princess Tanaquil, sitting in the window seat of her day chambers, heard the grand vizier's roar. Startled out of her reverie, she looked out the window in time to see the cloud of green smoke fading as it drifted out of Sihlirian's lair. She shuddered, knowing what it meant: he was practicing his dark arts again.

She had no love for her father's closest aide. He reminded her of a weasel, despite the aura of sorcerous power he wore like one of his rich cloaks. And ever since her thirteenth birthday, two months before, she had thrice caught him eyeing her with an odd expression – a combination of recognition and hatred – that would flee as soon as she noticed it.

As she wondered what cause Sihlirian might have to hate her, she felt a sudden pain in her heart. Instantly, she knew it had nothing to do with the grand vizier. This tasted of a different kind of authority – one underscored with love.

She ran to find her sisters. They were exactly where she expected them to be: in the sewing room next to the window, dressed in mourning for their mother, and chatting as they sewed garments for the poor. They turned to her as she entered, their smiles fading as they took in her breathless state.

Lissah, the eldest of the three, had dark curls and a serious air about her that made her seem older than her nineteen years. But her solemn exterior held a tender heart: she cared for her subjects as if they were her own children, and her heart broke when she saw them in distress. The sewing project had been her idea.

Lillah, at sixteen, was fair-haired and blue-eyed, and flirted outrageously with every man she met. Tanaquil often thought of them as an unmatched set, with Lissah taking after their father and Lillah taking after their mother.

And who did Tanaquil take after? She wished she knew, for she resembled neither of her parents. She was as tiny as they were tall, and olive-skinned where they were fair. And she knew things she had no normal way of knowing. She could still feel the lance of pain below her breastbone as she told her sisters in a rush, "We must go to Father. Something's happened."

Most in the castle either pooh-poohed Tanaquil's predictions or stayed far away from her. But her sisters, bless them, always believed her. In a trice, they had put aside their handiwork and rose to follow Tanaquil.

"What do you sense, Tannie?" Lissah asked as they hurried along the stone corridors to the king's receiving chamber. But Tanaquil had no breath to reply.

Rounding the final corner, the princesses skidded to a stop. The waiting area outside the receiving chamber was in an uproar.

"Clear the way!" announced Lissah, taking the lead and pushing her way through the throng of people. "We must see the king!"

But the guards at the door lowered their pikes to bar their way. "No one is to be admitted," the one on the left said.

"By whose order?" Lissah demanded.

"By order of the king's physician," he replied.

"Physician?" Lissah exclaimed, as Tanaquil's stomach clenched. The scene reminded her too much of the chaos surrounding their mother's death. She hoped their father yet lived.

Lillah had sidled up to the guard on the right. "I'm sure that stuffy old doctor didn't mean us, Nob," she said, fluttering her eyelashes at him. "After all, we're family."

Nob's grip on his pike wavered. "The princess has a point, " he said to his comrade.

"Oh, very well," said the guard on the left as he raised his weapon. The princesses flashed grateful smiles at them, opened the door, and slipped inside.

Tanaquil's worst fears were realized. Their father lay on the floor before his throne in a most undignified position, the royal physician kneeling at his side. The man looked up in surprise as the girls entered. "I told the guards no one was to be…oh. It's you." He rose and came toward them. "Your highnesses, I am sorry to inform you, but…."

Lissah and Lillah rushed to their father. Tanaquil stood frozen for a moment, taking in the tableau: her sisters sobbing as they knelt on either side of the king; the royal physician standing off to one side, looking useless. The pain in her heart that had called her here had vanished, replaced by a different, more familiar ache – one that seemed to say, in time with her heartbeat, *Too soon, too soon.*

She bent to drop a kiss on her father's cooling forehead. "Goodbye, Papa," she whispered, and fled – out the concealed door to one side of the chamber, down unused passages, and out a neglected gate in the curtain wall into sunshine. Still running, she made for the woods.

She had always gone to the woods to think, but more often since her mother's death a scant three months before. Nature salved her sore heart in a way nothing else could.

Even nature could not help her today. But still she ran. She had no objective, no destination in mind; all she wanted was to get away. Away from the simpering courtiers and their manufactured sympathy; away from her sisters' faces, limned anew in grief; away from the grand vizier, who even now, she was certain, was scheming to turn the tide of events to his favor.

So she was surprised when her feet drew up short at the gate of a charming cottage she had never seen before. Moreover, her gift told her she had business here; her hand moved toward the latch even before she could make herself presentable. Staying her hand for a moment, she swiped at her eyes with one black sleeve cuff. Then she righted her conical headdress, which had slid off her head and hung down her back, and brushed the dust off the trailing end of its veil. At last, she lifted the latch and let herself in.

A crow cawed loudly behind her; she turned as it flew over her, just brushing the tip of her hat and fluttering her veil. She ducked and put both hands to her headdress as her eyes followed the bird's path. With another cry, it landed on the shoulder of the amply padded woman in peasant garb who seemed to have materialized in front of the cottage door. "Gilbert!" the woman scolded the bird in a rich contralto. "No need to scare the lady." The woman inclined her head to Tanaquil. "Your highness."

"You know me," said the princess as she advanced toward the woman, "and yet you do not bow?"

The woman threw back her head and laughed, unsettling the crow from his perch. "I bow to no one, highness," the woman said, as Gilbert landed on her shoulder again. But she said it kindly, with twinkling eyes.

Despite the woman's insolence, Tanaquil found that she liked her. "And who are you, who bows to no one?"

"Call me Magaidh," the woman said, inclining her head.

Tanaquil inclined her head in turn. "I am honored to meet you."

That got another laugh out of the woman, unseating the crow yet again. He cawed and flapped away. "Oh, go along with you then,

Gilbert," Magaidh said, making shooing motions. "I don't need you for this transaction, anyway."

Tanaquil's eyes widened. "Transaction? But I have asked you for nothing. And you have nothing I need." She glanced around the neat garden.

"Oh, but I do," Magaidh said mysteriously. "Come inside, highness. I've just made tea. It will help ease your grief."

The word *grief* reminded the girl of the scene she had just fled. Despite the fresh blow, she schooled her features and said, "You judge my state by my raiment. Yet you speak of my grief as if it were fresh. Why?"

But the woman held open her door and said only, "Come inside, my dear."

She would have fled if her gift had not insisted that she hear the woman out. Warily, she allowed it to push her into the cottage.

Tanaquil had been in more peasants' hovels than the average princess. She and her sisters were devoted to good works on behalf of the common people of their kingdom, whose lot seemed to worsen even as that of the kingdom improved. But Magaidh's cottage was like no peasant's home she had ever seen. For one thing, it was flooded with light from some unseen source. Colorful rugs covered a real wooden floor, and a tea set of delicate Totol porcelain sat upon a table next to a window that overlooked...the sea? Tanaquil blinked. "You're a sorceress," she said to her hostess.

"A sorceress? Oh! You mean the window." Magaidh flicked her fingers, and the view shifted to the trees outside. "I fancied a bit of sea air this morning, that's all. Forgot to change it back when I was done breaking my fast." She bustled to the table and poured tea into the waiting cups, then eased herself onto one of the tiny chairs.

Tanaquil took the other chair and studied her hostess. "You have yet to answer my question," she said.

"News travels fast," Magaidh said, and sipped her tea. "Your father, the king, passed on not an hour since."

"How do you...?"

"And so close on the heels of the queen's death, too. Your sisters must be very sad indeed."

She wondered at the odd phrasing. "We all are." She lifted her cup and sniffed at the contents – chamomile and nothing else. Satisfied, she took a sip.

"The queen was a fine lady," Magaidh said. "Too good for the likes of your father."

Tanaquil put her cup down. "You knew my mother?"

"I know your mother," said Magaidh, with a little smile.

Another odd phrasing. Tanaquil tilted her head, puzzled.

"Truly, no one has ever told you?" Magaidh asked, and sighed. "Then I suppose it falls to me, lady. And who better than family?"

"Family?" This was getting stranger by the second.

"King Karolnu was your father," Magaidh said, dropping her voice, "but Queen Elinor was not your mother."

"Not…?" Tanaquil's head spun, and not from the tea. She stared out the window, not seeing the trees, as things slipped into place in her mind: why she did not resemble her sisters. Why she was the only one of the three with a gift. "Then my mother was a sorceress," she said slowly.

"*Is* a sorceress," said Magaidh. And when Tanaquil brought her eyes back into focus, the kindly peasant woman was gone. In her place was a slight, olive-skinned woman, her green eyes brimming with unshed tears.

"You…?" Tanaquil sat frozen for a moment. Then she nearly upset the tiny table in her rush to hug her own mother at last.

Gradually, over more cups of tea, the whole story came out. Fourteen years before, Karolnu had gone along with his troops on one of his foreign campaigns. Usually he left war to his generals, but Tanaquil knew he occasionally went along for the thrill of the battle. On this particular campaign, her father's troops were in the process of overrunning Magaidh's village when the king came upon some of his soldiers attempting to force themselves on her. He ordered them away – and took her for his concubine.

"He didn't know you were a sorceress," Tanaquil surmised.

"No – nor would he ever learn it," said Magaidh. She went on to explain that she had had a vision, many years before, that a child of hers would end a great injustice in the world. But she never married and had despaired of the prophecy ever coming true. Until that day. "When Karolnu learned I was with child," she went on, "he insisted on bringing me back here, to Nantulia. And all was well until I met that viper Sihlirian." Her eyes hardened in memory.

"He knew what you were."

"Immediately. And when I was delivered of the child – of you, my dear – he kidnapped me from my lying-in bed and tried to kill me."

Tanaquil shook her head. "I am not surprised at that. But you're not dead."

Magaidh gave her a cunning smile. "He thought he had killed me. But he was mistaken." She reached for Tanaquil's hand on the table and held it fast. "And he never knew of your gift. I made sure of that. I would have made my way home after my escape, except for you."

Tanaquil felt suddenly faint. "Your vision. You mean…?" She pulled out of Magaidh's grasp and held fast to the edge of the table. "But I cannot fight Sihlirian! I'm just a girl!"

Magaidh ignored her outburst. Fixing Tanaquil with the intensity of her stare, she said, "For thirteen years, I have bided my time, waiting for you to reach maturity, waiting for you to grow into your gift. The waiting is over. The time is now." She stood. "Come. We begin your training today."

Tanaquil began to babble in her panic. "But Father's funeral…and Lissah and Lillah will need me! They'll miss me. And Lissah will be…." She faltered.

Magaidh nodded. "That's right. Lissah will be queen. And she is not yet of age, so of course Sihlirian will insinuate himself into the position of regent – just as he did when your father's parents died." The tiny woman seemed to loom over Tanaquil. "All the wars, all the useless killing and plundering, all the resources wasted abroad while Nantulians go hungry at home – all of that will continue. Sihlirian will make sure of it. Lissah's heart is in the right place, but Sihlirian will turn her, just as he did your father. In six months, you will not know your sister."

The truth in Magaidh's words resonated in Tanaquil's heart. She released the table and stood. "What would you have me do?"

For a year and a day, Tanaquil served as apprentice under her mother Magaidh. She learned herb lore and animal lore, spells and cantrips, and scores of methods of divination. Her gift made her an apt student; she seemed to recall everything as soon as the knowledge was presented to her, as if she had known it already.

"You did, my dear," said Magaidh, when Tanaquil remarked on the phenomenon. "The knowing is passed down from mother to daughter. It only needed unlocking."

Tanaquil nodded as she reheated her cup of tea with a wave of her hand.

Among her lessons were some in the dark arts. Tanaquil drew back in revulsion when she realized what her mother was about. "I will not learn this," she declared. "It would make me no better than the Weasel."

"My dear child," said Magaidh, "you are already better than the Weasel." She had readily adopted Tanaquil's private term for the grand vizier. "The gift is in your bones – an advantage no man will ever have. Men must spend years learning what we know intrinsically, and therefore their knowledge will ever be incomplete." She stepped closer to Tanaquil, and lowered her voice. "But still, to defeat him, you must know what he knows. *All* of it."

And so the princess learned of torture and death, and of things worse than death. Her tender heart was dismayed to realize that this knowledge, too, was inherent in her, needing only to be unlocked. Her stomach rebelled more than once. But grimly, she held on – and was relieved to learn that she could defeat the dark arts without resorting to them herself.

Occasionally, her mother would send her on a quest. One bright winter morning, Magaidh kicked her out of the cottage with nothing but a shawl against the cold, and refused to let her back in until she had found her animal helper.

Tanaquil gave her a determined nod and set out along the path that led deeper into the woods. She had long since put aside her mourning dress – Magaidh had deemed it impractical for the study of her arts – and was dressed instead as a boy, in woolen trousers and a long-sleeved tunic. As she walked, she concentrated on connecting with the earth through her thin-soled shoes and wondered what form her helper would take. Gilbert the crow was a perfect match for her mother's wisdom. She rather fancied a bird for her own helper, but she knew the choice was not up to her.

Presently, her stomach began to rumble. After a short search, she found a cache of nuts in the crook of a tree, and apologized aloud to whatever animal had stored them as she took a handful. A bit of digging rewarded her with a couple of edible, albeit frozen, roots, and there was abundant snow to slake her thirst. She dusted snow off a log and sat down to enjoy her feast – and realized something was watching her from the shadows. Something with a sharp nose that was even now sniffing out the fruits of her foraging.

With a smile, she cracked open a few of the nuts. Then she dropped one behind her, and bent to adjust her shoe. Sure enough, she could hear the creature creep out of its hiding place and gulp down the nutmeat.

More? said a tiny voice in her head.

She sat up and turned. A fox was seated on the snow behind her, just out of reach.

Of course, she thought. She would need the fox's cunning to defeat the Weasel.

She shelled another couple of nuts and tossed them to her new friend, who gobbled them down and sat back on his haunches, grinning. "I'm Tanaquil," she said, as if she conversed with foxes every day.

Call me Theo, said the voice in her head.

She shelled the rest of the nuts and gave half of them to her new friend, together with one of the roots she had found. When she had finished her scanty repast, she stood. "Come on, Theo. Let's go back to the cottage so you can meet Magaidh." And she began walking back the way she had come, the fox trotting at her heels.

In early spring, Magaidh sent her out on another quest – this one for a type of onion called a rampion. "I need it for a particular project," Magaidh said. "I must have the very best. And that grows only in the garden of a nasty old woman who has enchanted the place. Only those of pure heart may enter."

"She's a witch," Tanaquil said.

Magaidh laughed. "No, my dear. You and I are witches. She's just a nasty old woman who knows a cantrip or two."

So early the next morning, Tanaquil and Theo set out for the nasty old woman's house.

It was a long walk. The woman dwelt beyond the village of Monfort – through the woods, over a river, and across a range of hills. Tanaquil was young and fleet of foot, but the trip still took the better part of three days. Still, there are worse things to endure than a three-day journey in early spring, when the trees are just leafing out and the meadow flowers are beginning to bloom.

Tanaquil realized that it had been nearly a year since her father's death. All at once, she longed to know what was going on at home – because even though Magaidh was her real mother and had been so kind to her, still she thought of the castle as her home. She wondered how Lissah was faring beneath the weight of the crown, with the Weasel guiding her – or, more accurately, with him telling her what to do.

She recalled Magaidh's prediction: that her sweet, serious sister would become a different person under Sihlirian's tutelage. Magaidh had given it six months. It had now been a year, or nearly so. Tanaquil both yearned to go home, and dreaded the changes she would find there. Would Lissah be cold and heartless to her? How would she treat her subjects? Was there still a Nantulia worthy of the name?

She knew that she was shortly to find out. Magaidh had often told her that her apprenticeship would last a year and a day. Soon, she would have to battle the Weasel. She would have to employ her knowledge of the dark arts to defeat him, without indulging in them herself. That was going to take cunning. She glanced down at Theo and said, "You'll help me defeat the Weasel, won't you, my friend?"

The fox looked up at her and grinned, his tongue lolling. *Weasels are fun to defeat*, he said in her head.

She smiled back. "Ah. But this one might be trickier than most."

Nevertheless, we will prevail. You are very tricky, and I am a fox.

She laughed. "I hope you're right, Theo." They were cresting the final range of hills before Monfort, and she paused to take in the view. Behind her, the hills they had traversed marched back into the distance. Before her, at the foot of the hills, lay a vast forest. Clearings dotted it here and there. The nearest, and largest, was Monfort. Beyond it, she saw a smaller break in the trees, and her gift told her she would find the nasty old woman's garden there.

She nodded to herself. "Standing here all day won't get the job done," she said to Theo, and began the hike to town.

As she picked her way down the hill, she stumbled. *Only the pure of heart may enter the garden*, Magaidh had said. What if she were no longer pure of heart? What if simply knowing the dark arts had taken her innocence away – even if she never intended to practice them?

Intent must mean something, she reasoned, else this would be a fool's journey. And Magaidh would never intentionally set her up to fail.

She righted herself and kept moving, although her steps were a little less confident than before.

It was a longer walk than it had appeared from her vantage point above the town. She did not reach the old woman's cottage until dusk. The cottage was unremarkable; it looked like any other peasant hovel she had ever seen in her travels with her father and sisters. But the garden, enclosed on all sides with a rickety fence, was unlike any she had ever seen: blooms of every hue and from every season; berry bushes loaded with fruit; tomatoes as big as two fists together. Even Magaidh's garden was not as prolific as this one.

Tanaquil wondered why the birds had not picked those berry bushes clean. Spring was so young that the wild bushes had not yet bloomed, let alone had time to set fruit. Something was very odd here. She and Theo hunkered down in the woods across the way to watch.

They did not have long to wait. An impetuous bird flew down from the trees and began to circle above the garden, as if looking for a way in. A moment later, a woman with a sour expression, her back bent nearly double with age, came out onto the porch and eased herself into a chair next to the door. The woman watched intently as the bird continued its circuit. At last, the bird swooped in and made for an ochreberry bush. There was a bang, and a flash so bright that Tanaquil hid her eyes against the glare. When she looked again, the bird lay, unmoving, next to the bush.

The old woman laughed uproariously. "Thought you could steal one of my ochreberries, did you? Thought one of 'em had your name on it, did you? I guess you've learned your lesson!" She got to her feet and hobbled to the garden, where she kicked the bird to make sure it was really dead. "Those are *my* berries! This is *my* garden! And not nobody nor nothing can get into it but *me!*" She used a trowel to scoop up the bird and toss it over the fence into the woods. Then she hobbled back toward her house, saying loudly, "No sir! Not nobody nor nothing gets over or through that fence but me!" But ten paces from the garden, she shrieked and turned back. "My parsnip!" she cried. "My best baby parsnip! How could it be gone?" She knelt with some difficulty next to a rather large hole and shook her fists at the sky. Then with a number of groans, she hoisted herself to her feet again and snatched up a straight stick next to the tomato plants. Going counter-clockwise around the outside of the fence, she muttered to herself, "Triple the height! Triple the strength! None shall pass this fence but me!"

As the woman worked, Tanaquil discerned a wall of sickly yellow – the color of fear and cowardice – ascend from the ground into the sky around the fence. Three times the old woman made the circuit, reciting her cantrip three times with each pass. When at last she was done, she replaced her wand next to the tomatoes, dusted off her hands, and said, "There. That oughta do it." Then she went back inside and slammed the door behind her.

"A nasty old woman indeed," Tanaquil murmured. She had thought to place a glamour on herself, much as her mother had done when they had first met, and appear as a hungry beggar to the woman. But she saw now that would be futile. Pure hearts had nothing to do with it; this was all about one woman's greed. She turned to Theo. "Something is getting in somehow," she said quietly. "Do you have any ideas how?"

I do, he said, his grin evident even in the near-dark. *She said over and through, but she never said anything about under.*

"That has to be it," she said, her hope restored. "Let's take a walk around that fence."

Sure enough, in a back corner, hidden amongst the roots of a tree, Theo spotted a hole. He stuck his pointed snout in it and sniffed. *Rabbit,* he told her. *And the scent is very fresh.* Without further adieu, he slipped into the hole. Tanaquil crouched behind the garden fence so that it blocked the view from the house and waited.

A few minutes later, Theo emerged from the hole, panting. *I got to the garden without tripping the cantrip,* he said, *but the rampion is rooted fast. I can't pull it out by myself. You will have to come, too.*

Tanaquil looked doubtfully at the hole. "I can't fit through that."

I know. I'll make it bigger. And he began digging at the hole with his front paws.

The excavation project took most of the night. Dawn was breaking as the pair emerged from the hole, tired and sweaty despite the chill in the air. Tanaquil tried her best to imitate Theo's flowing movements as they sneaked across the garden to the rampion patch. She could see the teeth marks in the one her companion had tried to pull. No wonder he had failed – the rampion was the size of a small watermelon. But she and Theo took hold, and with a mighty pull, the thing broke free of the earth with a *rrrip!* Tanaquil landed on her rear with the massive rampion in her lap. Up she scrambled as Theo bounded toward the hole and freedom.

As she reached the tunnel, she heard a click, and glanced back. The cottage door was opening. "Go!" she hissed, although Theo was already out the other side. She rolled the huge onion into the tunnel ahead of her – and it stuck against a tree root, inches from freedom.

"My rampion!" the nasty old woman wailed.

"Theo! Pull!" Tanaquil cried. She felt him began to tug on the rampion as she put her shoulder into it from behind. With a shower of dirt, the rampion broke free.

"Thief! Thief!" the old woman yelled. "That's *my* rampion!"

Tanaquil popped out on the far side of the tunnel. "Not any more," she called, and flicked her fingers at her. "And from this day, missus, you will no longer deprive any birds or animals of your garden's bounty!"

The woman reeled as if physically struck. Then she sagged. "I will share," she said dully. "I don't know what got into me. I've always shared before." She dismissed the cantrip surrounding her garden with a wave; Tanaquil saw the sickly yellow walls fall. Then the old woman turned and shuffled back into her house.

Tanaquil stuffed the rampion into her rucksack. Then she and Theo began the long hike home.

As she walked, she thought. And thought some more. And so it was that when they reached Magaidh's cottage at last, the first thing she said after she dropped the rampion on the tea table was this: "You tricked me."

"I did not," said Magaidh as she scooped up the rampion and bustled into the kitchen with it.

Tanaquil followed her. "You cursed that poor old woman."

"It wasn't a curse," said Magaidh. "My, this is a big one."

"You placed a spell on her, then," Tanaquil said. "So that she would hoard her produce. So that I would have to figure out how to snatch the rampion from her."

"That I did." Magaidh reached for her longest knife.

"Why?" Tanaquil shouted. "She was killing *birds,* Magaidh! And anything else that tried to get in!"

"Mm-hmm," said Magaidh absently. "And she would have killed you, too, if you hadn't figured out how to get in without tripping the spell."

Tanaquil took a step back. "I thought you loved me," she said in a small voice.

Magaidh put down the knife and turned to face Tanaquil. "I do," she said. "With every fiber of my being. But Sihlirian does not, and your battle with him is nearly at hand. You need to know how to size up an opponent. How to discover his weaknesses, and how to exploit those weaknesses. Before he finds and exploits yours." She picked up the knife again and, with a mighty swing, cleft the rampion in two.

When she turned again to her daughter, there were tears in her eyes. "You are young, and quick, and you have the knowledge in your bones. But you are also inexperienced. Sihlirian will know that, and he will try to exploit it."

"So I will make my inexperience a strength," said Tanaquil, her voice gaining strength with every word she spoke. "He will think me an unworthy opponent, a mere bug to be crushed under his heel. I will surprise him."

A tear slid from the corner of Magaidh's eye. "I hope so, my dear. For far more is at stake than birds and onions." She dashed the moisture from her cheek with the back of one hand and picked up the knife again.

"What do you need the rampion for, anyway?" Tanaquil asked.

"Lunch," said Magaidh. "Would you please get some lettuce from the garden, dear?"

Two days more, and Tanaquil's apprenticeship was done.

She stood on her mother's threshold, dressed again in mourning and that absurd veiled hat. She should no longer need to wear black, but it was the only attire she had that was appropriate for court. "I will have to sneak into my chamber and change, lest someone think something is amiss," she told Magaidh as she straightened her cuffs.

"Although I suppose my reappearance after a year will be strange, no matter how I'm dressed."

"Don't worry about your dress," her mother said. "It may matter less than you think."

She glanced at Magaidh sharply, but the woman seemed serene enough. So she embraced her and kissed her cheek. "I will be back to visit," she said.

"Of course you will. And I will be with you every step of the way. In here." Magaidh tapped Tanaquil's temple. "And in here." She placed her hand over her daughter's heart. For a moment Tanaquil held it fast, saying all with her eyes that her lips could not find a way to express. Then she let herself out at the gate and began the walk back to the castle with Theo at her heels.

She sneaked back in through the neglected gate in the curtain wall, surprised to find it still open, and made her way through the hidden passageways to her chamber, where she left Theo. Or tried to. "You shall be safe here," she told him.

No, he said. *My place is with you.*

So together, they made their way to the anteroom outside the throne room – where she found all in chaos.

Fear clutched her heart. *Not Lissah, too!* She approached the guards by the door and asked, "What has happened here?"

The men looked at her in consternation. "But…but highness," Nob stammered, "you and your sisters entered just a minute ago. How did you get out here?"

Twin wails of grief erupted from behind the door.

"Let me in," she ordered the guards, who obeyed with alacrity.

Inside the room, she blinked in disbelief. There was her father, prone on the floor before the throne; there were Lissah and Lilleh, kneeling beside him; there was the royal physician, looking useless; and there on the right, the tapestry that hid the secret passage entrance waved slightly, as if someone had recently ducked through the door.

Somehow, her mother had managed to compress her year-and-a-day apprenticeship into a mere few seconds.

While all eyes were on her father's body, she strode to the moving tapestry and opened the door. A pointed snout stuck through the crack. She pulled the door open further and murmured, "You are tricky, Theo."

I am a fox, he agreed. *And here comes the Weasel.*

She left the door open and emerged from behind the tapestry just as Sihlirian entered from the anteroom.

He looked even oilier than she remembered. His gaze took in the scene; she could almost hear the gears turning in his head, weighing his options for taking the best advantage of the situation. For a moment, his eyes rested on her. In return, she looked steadily back at him. He seemed momentarily befuddled, as if he were trying to place her. Then he rubbed his forehead and his gaze slid away.

She schooled her features into an expression of sadness, but inwardly, she exulted. Her mother's glamour was still in place. He did not know who he was dealing with. But he would, and soon.

"What is going on here?" the grand vizier demanded of the royal physician.

"I regret to inform you, sir," the physician began, "but...."

Sihlirian held up one gloved hand, and the physician's words died in his throat. Crossing to the tableau of grief, he made a show of removing his feathered hat while he took a knee at her father's feet. "My liege," he murmured sorrowfully, loud enough for all in the chamber to hear. "Dearest Karolnu. Gone too soon, just as your parents before you." He rested there a moment, gazing at her father. Then he turned his gaze to Lissah and bowed before her. She regarded him numbly as he said, "My queen, I know it is too soon, but it cannot be helped. Someone must take charge of arrangements for your father's lying in state and burial, and for your coronation. And as your regent...."

Tanaquil stepped forward to stand next to her father's head. "Hold a moment, grand vizier. You are not regent yet."

The Weasel looked up at her, frowning. Then he got to his feet. "Your pardon, highness, but perhaps your grief has muddled your understanding of what has transpired. Your sister has inherited the throne, yet she is too young to serve without a regent – and your mother, bless her memory, is no longer with us. I have a long record of service to the family," he went on, warming to the subject, "first as regent to your father, and then as his most trusted adviser. Who better to be your sister's regent?" He spread his arms wide. "Who else is there?"

"I don't know yet," Tanaquil said evenly, "but there must be someone better than you."

Lissah rose to her feet gracefully, tears still shining on her cheeks. "Tannie," she said, "perhaps this should wait for a better time."

"No," she said, keeping her eyes trained on Sihlirian. "This must be done now, Lissah. Before he can sink his claws into you."

Lissah gasped. But Lilleh said, "She's right, Lissie." She got to her feet and planted herself with her arms crossed. "If he's in charge, we'll never make the changes we have been yearning to make. Our people will continue to go hungry while *he*" – she stabbed a forefinger at the Weasel – "keeps lining his own pockets."

"Now, highness," Sihlirian said, raising both hands as if to forestall her. "You misunderstand."

"We misunderstand nothing," Tanaquil said. "Nantulia has had thirty-five years of your kind of governing. It needs to end now – before the people revolt."

"Have a care, highness," the Weasel growled. "Recall who you are talking to."

"I know exactly who I'm talking to, grand vizier," she shot back. "*You* are the one in the dark." She snapped her fingers and the lights went out. She gave it a moment, so everyone could make their exclamations of surprise and dismay. Then she snapped her fingers again, and held her palm out before her. A tiny flame danced there, shedding just enough light to illuminate the faces of her sisters and the Weasel.

Lissah and Lilleh's mouths had formed Os of surprise. The Weasel, however, was not so easily entranced. "A nice cantrip, highness," he sneered. "Did you buy it at the fair?"

"I did not," Tanaquil said, refusing to rise to his bait. "My mother taught me."

"Mother…?" said Lilleh.

"Mother didn't know any magic," said Lissah.

"My *real* mother taught me," said Tanaquil. "Magaidh of Totollia."

Realization dawned on Sihlirian's face. "You," he said.

"Me," said Tanaquil with a nod. She flicked a finger and the room brightened slowly.

"You lie," the Weasel said, recovering. "Magaidh of Totollia is dead."

Tanaquil gave him an arch smile. "Is she? Are you certain?" She snapped her hand into a fist, extinguishing the flame. "She looked quite healthy to me when we parted this morning."

"She bewitched me," he growled. "She made me believe…." He stood, fuming, for a moment. "She must be found! Guards!"

"Belay that," ordered Lissah, standing tall, looking every inch the queen. "I have no quarrel with Magaidh. She was always kind to me."

"And to me," said Lilleh. "You, on the other hand, grand vizier…."

Sihlirian took in the three young, angry faces before him, and his brow lowered further. "I will not lose my place in this kingdom to three teenaged girls!" he said. "I'll see all of you hang for sedition! Guards!" he roared, and raised one hand as if to smite them.

A shadow raced across the room and jumped at Sihlirian's throat. The man went down hard, screaming and clawing at his attacker, as Theo bit him repeatedly.

"Highness!" the royal physician cried, shaking Tanaquil's shoulder. "Call off the fox! It will tear out his throat!"

She had forgotten the man was there. She turned to him, shrugged, and turned back to watch Theo and his prey.

The guards rushed in seconds later, but the deed was done. Two dead men now lay on the throne room floor: King Karolnu and Sihlirian. The grand vizier's blood soaked into the exquisitely-patterned Cartagelian rug.

As the guards took both bodies away, the royal physician hurrying along behind them, Lilleh shook her head at the stain. "Father always liked that rug," she said. Then her face crumpled.

The three sisters hugged one another and cried. Tanaquil, who had had a year to get used to her father being gone, realized her own tears were of relief. It was over. Sihlirian was gone. Life would be better for every Nantulian from now on.

At length, the girls drew back from one another. "I still need a regent," said Lissah, blotting at her eyes with a handkerchief. "Tannie, do you suppose you could ask Magaidh?"

Tanaquil beamed. "My liege, it would be my pleasure." She looked past Lissah at Theo, who grinned up at her from his place on the rug. She could see the reddish smears where had wiped his muzzle. *Tricky Theo,* she thought, and hoped he could hear her. *You did well, my friend.*

I told you, he said. *Weasels are fun to defeat.*

Forever Blowing Bubbles

Since we're on the subject of coming-of-age stories, here's the one I wrote for Summer Dreams, *which was published in the summer (appropriately enough) of 2014. And once again, a pagan god provided me with a bit of inspiration.*

The bubbles got her attention.

The first one landed next to her book. She saw the iridescent glimmer out of the corner of her eye as it made its descent from behind her and popped on a blade of grass. She shrugged mentally and went back to her book.

The second one danced in on a languid breeze and landed on her open page. By some miracle of surface tension, it didn't pop right away. It sat there, slightly flattened on the bottom, and shimmied for a few seconds before popping. Irritated, she flicked at imaginary moisture on the page and went back to reading. She had bought the book – a fantasy by her favorite author – at Christmastime and set it aside to use as a reward to herself for finishing the semester. Now it was June and she finally had time to savor it. But someone was trying to wreck her concentration.

The third bubble popped on her nose. It was accompanied by a man's soft laughter. Scowling, she looked around, and spotted the culprit immediately. "Do you mind?" she said, not caring that her annoyance showed. "I'm trying to read here."

"I know," the man with the bubble wand said. "What I don't understand is why. You've had your nose in one book or another for months, and here it is – a beautiful summer's day – and the first thing you do is stick your nose in another book."

His words, with their implication that he'd been watching her, would have troubled her more if they had been coming from someone else. But the Bubble Man was silver-haired, with the large nose and ears of the very old. One ear sported a hearing aid. He was smiling at her in an open, friendly way – not creepy at all.

She closed her novel and pushed herself up from her prone position. Sitting with her legs crossed, she squinted up at him. "Do I know you?"

"Not yet," he said with laughter in his voice. He didn't sound old, she noticed; his voice was strong and deep. "The name's Lou." He reached out a hand; automatically, she shook it.

"I'm Darcy," she said.

"I know."

"Look," she said. "What's this about? You sounded like a stalker a minute ago."

He laughed outright. "No, no, no," he said. "You have nothing to fear from me. I'm here to help you."

"Uh-huh."

"C'mon. Let me buy you a soda and I'll explain." He hooked a thumb at the refreshment stand across the street. Against her better judgment, she nodded.

"What's got you so het up about finishing that book of yours?" he asked as they headed up the sidewalk.

She hefted the thick novel. "I've been dying to read it since it came out last fall, but I put it off 'til now so it wouldn't interfere with my studies. And I've only got two weeks to get it done."

Lou snorted. "Some pleasure reading. What happens in two weeks?"

"Summer session starts. I'll be hard at work again."

He stopped in the middle of the path. "But you just got out of school! And it was a tough semester, too. Wasn't it?"

"Yeah, it was," she said. "Two math classes and physiology, too. But I need to retake organic chemistry, and I'd rather get it out of the way over the summer."

He began walking again, and she followed him. "You flunked organic chemistry?" he asked with a sidelong glance.

"Not exactly," she said, turning red as she remembered the C she had received. "But I know I can do better. And my grades have to be perfect so I can get into med school."

"Hmm. So your classmates are spending their summer in school, too, I guess."

She frowned. "I don't think so."

"Then they got perfect grades."

She snorted. "Hardly."

"So then this is about you," he said. "Why are you being so hard on yourself?"

She gave him an incredulous look. "Because I want to be a doctor."

He shook his head. "I understand that. But your classmates do, too, and they're not spending their summer hitting the books."

"Maybe they're smarter than me," she muttered. *Or came to college better prepared.* She'd been a star in high school, but that wasn't saying much. Her inner-city school didn't exactly challenge its students. She had spent her whole first two years of college feeling stupid.

"You don't believe that," he scoffed. "You're plenty smart, Darcy. And you'll make a fine doctor. You just need to believe in yourself."

She felt as if she'd been caught out. Of course she didn't believe in herself. She'd been brought up to expect disappointment. "Easy for you to say," she told him. "You don't have your whole family waiting on you to fail."

He regarded her with a sympathetic look. "Come on. Let's get that soda." And he stepped off the curb.

"Lou! Look out!" she yelled over the screech of brakes.

The car swerved, but clipped him on the leg. The impact sent him sprawling onto the sidewalk, his head smacking the concrete with a sickening thud.

"Oh, my God!" the driver cried. She had pulled over and was now hovering over the fallen man. "Is he okay?"

Darcy spared her barely a glance. "Call 911," she said brusquely, as she knelt next to her new friend. He was unconscious, but breathing. That was something, at least. Quickly, she checked him over – he wore no medic alert bracelet and his pupils constricted normally. The back of his head was bloody where he'd landed, and his leg was beginning to swell at the point of impact.

She glanced up at the driver, who was still standing over them. "I need to call my mom," the girl said. "Oh, my God. I didn't mean to hit him."

"Did you call 911?" Darcy asked. Then, belatedly, "Are you okay?"

"I didn't mean to hit him," she said again. She crossed her arms over her chest and began rubbing her upper arms.

She's in shock. Darcy rose and put one hand on her forearm, stilling the movement. "Of course, you didn't mean to," she said kindly. "Why don't you have a seat on the grass."

"Okay," the girl said. Darcy slipped her sweater from her bag and threw it over the girl's shoulders. Then she went back to Lou.

The next few minutes passed in a blur. Reflecting later, Darcy thought it was as if something clicked in her head – a switch she hadn't known existed until the crisis occurred. She directed someone in the gathering crowd to call 911 as she triaged both patients. And when the paramedics came, she gave them an efficient report and handed the situation over to them.

"He'll be fine," one of the paramedics told her, as they were loading Lou into the ambulance. "The doc in the E.R. just wants to check him over. Good thing you were here. Are you a paramedic?"

Darcy shook her head. "Pre-med."

"Good choice," he told her. "You'll make a great doc."

"I will?" she asked in surprise. But he had already turned away, and the noise of the ambulance's motor drowned her out.

As he got in the ambulance, though, he turned back to her. "Call me if you ever decide to become a paramedic," he yelled. "We could use you."

She couldn't get the events of that day out of her head. Every time she picked up her novel, she remembered the bubbles, and what had happened afterward.

The day after the accident, she called the hospital to check on both Lou and the young driver, but the receptionist said the information Darcy had wasn't enough to find them in her system.

Three days later, she received a bouquet. The card read, "I told you you could do it. Have a great summer." It was signed, "Lugh."

The odd spelling sent her to the Internet, where she learned Lugh was the name of an Irish god. Apparently, Lugh the god could do anything.

Even, maybe, appear to a pre-med student as a bubble-blowing old man with a hearing aid?

She dismissed the fanciful notion as soon as it occurred to her. She was trained to think rationally – too rationally to believe that some deity might appear to her out of the blue. Magic only happened in books, after all.

But the next day, she dropped her summer class. Then she went back to the park. And on the way, she bought herself a bottle of bubble water.

A Man's Got to Do What a Man's Got to Do

This story was written as blatant self-promotion for the Pipe Woman Chronicles, my urban fantasy series. Alan was kind enough to publish it in 13 Bites Vol. 1. For those of you playing along at home, this story is set a few years before the events in Seized, the first book. At one point in the series, Joseph's pal George tells Naomi that he had seen Joseph shapeshift only once. Here's how it happened.

"I hate these things," George complained, squinting at himself in the mirror. His war-painted visage squinted murderously back at him. "I feel like one of the Village People."

"Except that guy wasn't a real Indian," Joseph said as he leaned against the bathroom door frame, "and you are."

The feathered chief's headdress began to slip off the back of George's head. He caught it with one meaty hand, his scowl deepening. "How did our forefathers keep these things on their heads, anyhow? Why didn't they fall off while they were riding horses and kicking Lakota ass?"

"They tied them on really tight. Here, let me help you."

"Not a chance." George transferred his glare to his roommate. "Where's *your* costume, anyhow? I'm not gonna be the only one making a fool of myself at this thing tonight. Going to this party was your idea."

"Hold on just a second, pard," Joseph said, his deep blue eyes dancing. "I'm the one who got the invitation. But it was your idea to go. *You're* the one who's sweet on Valerie."

"I said she was cute once. Once." George shook a forefinger at his roommate. He gave his image a final glare, turned to leave the bathroom, and stopped. Joseph was still blocking the door. "Do you mind?"

Joseph grinned and stepped out into the hallway, one arm gesturing grandly. Valerie was a classmate of his at Metro State

University. She threw a costume party every October, or so she had said when she passed out the invitations. Her parents owned an old Victorian in Denver's Capitol Hill neighborhood – the perfect, creepy setting for a Halloween bash.

George stopped in front of Joseph. "No, really," he said. "Where's your costume?" At Joseph's widening smirk, his mouth dropped open. "Oh, no. You wouldn't. Not after you promised Looks Far."

Joseph reddened, but he raised his chin. "First," he said evenly, "I didn't promise I wouldn't ever shift again – just that I wouldn't do it as often."

"That's not how I heard it," George muttered.

"And second," Joseph went on, a little louder, "I'm not going to shift all the way for the party."

George ignored this last qualifier. "Do you really think that's smart? After last time?"

Joseph rolled his eyes and sighed. He couldn't pretend that he didn't know what George was talking about; George had been right there when the farmer had mistaken Joseph for a coyote come to raid his chicken coop, and almost shot him. To be fair, the farmer was only partly mistaken. Joseph had been a coyote – he just didn't have any interest in the man's chickens.

Both George and Joseph were Ute Indians, but Joseph was a skinwalker – someone who could assume the shape of nearly any other animal. Only a few people knew of his ability: his grandfather, Looks Far; George; and the elders of the reservation in Utah where Joseph and his grandfather used to live. The tribal controversy that had erupted over Joseph's shifting ability was one of the reasons why he and his grandfather no longer lived on the rez.

The other reason had to do with a vision his grandfather had received from a Lakota Sioux goddess, about a girl who would help bring the Indian nations power again. Joseph had promised himself that he would find that girl. But so far, he'd had no luck.

None of which had anything to do with the party tonight. He gave George a withering look and said, "I am always careful."

George snorted. "Yeah. You feed that same line to Looks Far. And he buys it every time, too." He shook his head. "If you're ready, let's go."

Joseph had a great time walking around the party, trying to pick out his classmates and watching their guarded reactions to him. In the suit and tie that he'd picked up at the ARC Thrift Store on West Colfax, he looked normal enough from the neck down. It was his head that confused people. He had tried to get it to the right proportions so that it looked like he had donned a mask, but he knew it wasn't quite right – the skull was too flat, the nose way too long, the tongue and teeth just a little bit too real. As long as he kept his larynx human, he could approximate his normal speaking voice. But the balance was taking a toll on his self-control. Coyote, who had bestowed upon him the ability to shapeshift, loved a party and wanted to take over. Joseph was beginning to think this "costume" had been a bad idea.

And then he caught sight of George talking to a strange Hispanic woman, and he *knew* it had been a bad idea. She was brown-skinned and blond-haired, with a generous but well-shaped figure, and she was dressed as a vampire: a black bolero and pants, and a blood-red cape. Her pointy teeth flashed as she spoke earnestly to George, with one hand on his wrist. Then her head whipped around as if she'd been stung, and eyes as red as her cape bored straight into Joseph.

He knew she wasn't fully human, any more than he was a coyote. Moreover, he was certain she knew *his* secret, too.

She whispered something in George's ear; as Joseph watched in trepidation and disgust, her tongue darted out to lick his earlobe. He joined his friend swiftly, but the woman was already gone, leaving George staring after her as if in a trance.

"Yo, George," Joseph said, waving his hand in front of his roommate's face. "Earth to George. Earth to George. Who was that?"

"Dolores," George said without turning his head. "She said her name was Dolores."

Joseph knew enough Spanish to know that wasn't good. "Hey," he said lightly, "did you talk to Valerie?"

George shook his head slightly and focused on Joseph. "Oh. Yeah, I did. She's cute."

"But did you ask her out?"

"I didn't get a chance to," George said. "Dolores butted into the conversation." He turned and looked after the woman again.

Joseph didn't like the way this was going. "Look, pard, let's go home," he said. "We've got an early start tomorrow." Both men worked construction. This week, they were on a job in Evergreen, on the other side of the city from their trailer. "I'll drive," Joseph offered, holding out his hand for the keys to the truck.

That snapped George out of it. "Oh, no, you won't," he said. "What if you see a jackrabbit and decide to take off after it? *I'll* drive."

On the way home, George's periodic sighing began to irritate Joseph. Finally, he said, "All right, tell me. What's got you all worked up?"

"I think she's in trouble."

"Who? Valerie?"

George took his eyes off the road for a second to stare at him. "No. Dolores."

"Oh?" Joseph tried to sound nonchalant. "What kind of trouble is she in?"

"It's not her, exactly. It's her brother. I guess he has a ranch out east of here." George gestured vaguely toward his right. "She said he's been having some trouble with his livestock."

"What kind of trouble?"

George laughed self-consciously. "It's gonna sound crazy, but she said a few of them have been turning up every morning dead. Drained of blood. With two puncture wounds in the neck."

Joseph turned to him, one eyebrow raised. "And she thinks her brother has a vampire on his hands?" With a smirk, he added, "Maybe she's the vampire."

"No," said George, as if he hadn't heard the last part of Joseph's comment. "Not a vampire. A chupacabra."

Now it was Joseph's turn to laugh. "Oh, come on! Chupacabras aren't real! They're mythical creatures!"

George turned to regard him with a serious expression. "So are you."

Joseph had to concede the point. After a moment, he said, "Why did she bother to tell you all of this, though?"

"She wants us to help her catch the thing."

"*Us?*"

"Yeah. Us. She specifically said, 'you and your friend.'" He glanced over at Joseph again. "Think it's a setup?"

"I *know* it's a setup," Joseph said, shuddering at the memory of the woman's eyes. "The question is why." He gazed out into the darkness. "I need to talk to Grandfather."

"I don't know much about the chupacabra," Looks Far told them. The Ute shaman was cooking steaks for their dinner on a grill outside his wickiup, after the younger men had helped him conduct a sweat lodge ceremony for a group of tourists. Joseph and George had helped him with his business since they were teenagers, and the old man always made them dinner afterward. *Payment for services rendered,* he would say with a solemn wink.

"Well, what *do* you know?" Joseph asked.

Looks Far shrugged. He wore a corduroy jacket against the chill, but his long, gray hair flowed free in the breeze. "The creature is supposed to be four or five feet long, with leathery skin like a reptile and spikes along its spine. It makes puncture wounds in the neck – either two or three, depending on who's telling the story – and sucks the animal's blood out through them."

"But it doesn't eat the carcass," George said.

"Not the way I heard it, no," Looks Far said.

"Nice," George said. Then his expression changed. "But we have to help her," he said, a faraway tone in his voice.

Looks Far gave George a searching look. "What exactly does this woman want you boys to do?"

"She said she wants us to help her catch it."

"And do what with it?"

George looked at the ground, the faraway look gone. "She didn't say."

Looks Far turned to Joseph for an explanation. "She's not human, Grandfather," Joseph said. "He's been doing this ever since she touched him at the party. Snapping in and out like this."

George looked at them in surprise. "I have?" His expression hardened.

"And her eyes were red," Joseph went on, putting a hand on his friend's shoulder.

Looks Far shrugged as he flipped the steaks. "That could have been a trick of the light."

Joseph shook his head. "I don't think so. I got the distinct feeling that she was something other than human. And what's more, she knew I was, too."

That brought the old man's head up fast. "She knows you're a skinwalker?"

"I don't know that she knows that much," Joseph said. "I just had a very strong feeling that she knew I wasn't a normal guy."

Looks Far glanced between his grandson and George. "And she asked for both of you to help her."

George nodded grimly.

The old man looked sideways at his grandson. "And you're going to rise to the bait, aren't you?"

Joseph bristled inwardly. But he plastered a grin on his face and said, "Sure. After all, Grandfather, you always told me that the best defense is a good offense. I think those steaks are about done, don't you?"

Joseph was still chafing at his grandfather's question when he and George got back to their trailer that night. "I'm going to go for a run," he said.

George hadn't known the two of them, grandfather and grandson, for so many years for nothing. "He didn't mean anything by it. You know that."

"Right."

"He thinks the world of you, Joseph. He's always been proud of you."

"Except for the shifting."

"Well, yeah."

"I'm going for a run," Joseph said again.

George sighed. "All right. Just...be careful."

Joseph's brow lowered. "Now you sound like him. Don't wait up for me."

"Oh, there's no danger of that, pard. I'm bushed. See you in the morning." And he headed off down the hall to his bedroom.

As soon as Joseph heard George's door shut, he stripped off his clothing and stepped outside into the cold night air. He shivered once, and then he shifted.

A moment later, Joseph Coyote bounded across the plains as fast as he could run.

For uncounted minutes, he reveled in unthinking movement. Shifting, for him, was both curse and coping mechanism; the call of his animal nature was always strongest when he was confused or upset. He didn't actually think through his problems when he was in another form – he couldn't, really. Tapping into his human nature while shifted was possible, but difficult; it took something away from his animal, so that it was impossible to be either one fully. But shifting usually cleared his head, allowing him to work out his emotional response in physical exertion, so that he could handle the situation rationally when he was human again.

By the time he had run a good ten miles and investigated all the prairie dog burrows in the neighborhood, he was starting to feel as if he could go home and sleep. But as he turned to begin the journey back, he felt the hairs rise along his spine. Something was moving in the tallgrass to his left. He crouched low, resisting the urge to growl, and waited.

It didn't take long.

The thing that rose slowly from the grass was big – bigger than he had been led to believe it would be. Its head, silhouetted against the rising moon, was shaped like a lizard's. When it turned its head from side to side, tasting the air with its tongue, he could see spikes running along its backbone. But its throat looked vulnerable to Joseph Coyote. Still he waited. Better to hide and fight another day, if need be.

Then the beast's red-hot eyes found him. Emitting a hiss, it came down on all fours and galloped toward him with frightening speed.

Joseph waited until the thing was nearly on him. Then he sprang, opening his jaws wide and aiming for the throat.

He connected. But his teeth could not penetrate the scaly hide. His jaw muscles throbbing, he swerved and dodged the monster's claws. Then he made a run for it.

Coyotes can run pretty fast when rested. But it was late in the day and he had already had a good run; now the thing was matching him, stride for stride. He felt himself tiring, and it scared him. He could think of only one way out. Dropping to his belly, he shifted once more.

A red-tailed hawk shot up from the place where the coyote had dropped.

A split second later, the monster pounced on the spot where it had seen the coyote go down.

Joseph circled the scene from a comfortable height to watch. At first, the beast bounced back in surprise when it came up empty-clawed. It threw its head back and uttered a bone-chilling wail of frustration. And then it saw him. Its eyes smoldered like live coals as it watched him ride the night air currents. Joseph realized belatedly that he was silhouetted against the moon; he flew some distance west, to put the monster between the moon and him, before alighting in a tree to watch the scene play out.

He could see the monster crouch, hiding in the tallgrass again. But it couldn't stay there forever; the sun would be up eventually, and this thing was clearly a creature of the night. So after a few minutes, it slunk away, heading east.

Joseph waited until he lost sight of it, alert to the possibility that it was circling to attack from another direction. Finally, satisfied he would be as safe as he ever was, he flew home. But he couldn't get the creature's fiery eyes – so like Dolores's – out of his mind.

"The thing is definitely after me, Grandfather," Joseph told the old man by phone during his coffee break the next day. He was having trouble staying focused on the job – it was nearly dawn when he got to bed, and then he couldn't fall asleep because he kept reliving the attack on the plains. He described it now to Looks Far, and then said, "I'm sure that girl who approached George at the party has something to do with it."

"How is George this morning?"

Joseph blew out a breath. "Back to normal. Whatever compulsion she put on him seems to be gone." He realized, as he spoke, what that meant. *The only thing she needed George for was to draw me into this.*

The old man sighed, apparently coming to the same conclusion. "If it is truly after you, Joseph, then you have no choice. You must go after it."

Joseph's lip curled. *Thanks for finally admitting I was right.*

"When are you and George meeting this girl?" Looks Far asked.

"Tomorrow. George has the address. We're supposed to drive out there in the afternoon and wait for it to show up." He shuddered involuntarily. He was not looking forward to meeting the monster again.

"And how do you plan to capture it?"

Joseph had been thinking about it. "If it's a shifter, then it must have only one alternate form – or it would have shifted again to try to catch me. So I have an advantage there. And I've seen what it can do. It's fast, but I was tired last night by the time it spotted me. I think I can outrun it if I'm fresh. So I think I can lead it into a trap. Then we can drop a net over it, or get a rope on it, or something, and wait for it to change back."

"You'll have to protect George."

"Of course. And the girl."

Looks Far paused for a moment before he said. "Yes. Of course."

Joseph knew what the pause meant. The memory of two pairs of red eyes had come back to him in a rush. "I know what you're thinking, Grandfather, and I think you might be right."

"Just make sure you're not the one who ends up trapped," the old man finally said.

"Man, this place is in the middle of nowhere," George said.

"Yeah." Joseph glanced at the passenger side mirror, in which the Rockies were rapidly growing smaller behind them. He asked himself again, for perhaps the hundredth time that day, why he was following through on this.

Joseph considered himself a good man, albeit with an unusual talent.   But he'd had enough experience with the supernatural over the past twenty-five years to know that if such a creature found him, it would keep tracking him down until he met the challenge – and sometimes it meant a fight to the death.

He'd been lucky so far. He'd survived.

So far.

He mourned each life he ended, though, and he always asked the gods to be kind to their troubled spirits as they began their long journey to the next world. But he never talked about this aspect of his existence with anyone. How could he? He was an extraordinary creature who sometimes had to kill other extraordinary creatures. No mere human, he felt, would understand the necessity. And no mere human could understand the toll it took on him to end a life so unique – one so much like his own.

At his lowest – which didn't happen often, but it did happen – he thought maybe it would be better just to let the next monster win.

But he had a powerful incentive to keep himself alive: he needed to track down White Buffalo Calf Pipe Woman's Indian savior. Looks Far had been a respected medicine man before he had had that vision; a lot of that respect disappeared with his insistence that it was true. Joseph intended to make sure his grandfather's honor was restored. They thought they had found the girl about twenty years back, but then she fell off their radar. Joseph promised himself that when this skirmish was over, he would try again to find her.

Which meant he had to survive.

"How much farther?" he asked.

George glanced at the GPS on the dashboard. "Next exit. Then about fifteen miles."

Joseph grunted. He kept from drumming his fingers on the door frame by forcing himself to inspect the landscape, scouring it for a natural feature they could use as a backstop for their makeshift corral: a rock outcropping, a pond, anything.

George glanced at him as he navigated the exit from I-70. "Seen anything we could use?"

"No," Joseph said shortly. "You?"

"Not yet." George paused. "What are we gonna do if we can't find something?"

Joseph shrugged. "Farm's gotta have a barn."

"You think a barn will hold that thing?"

He met George's eyes. "Maybe not. But if it's all we've got, it's all we've got."

It was George's turn to grunt. Joseph went back to sizing up the passing fields. Presently, he said, "What if we stack those hay bales?"

"With what? You know how heavy the round ones are."

"I could shift. A bear could handle them, I bet."

"And draw the thing right to us before we're ready."

Joseph glanced at his friend. "Damn it, I hate it when you're right. Have you got a better idea?"

"I wish I did," George said, signaling a left onto a dirt road, even though they hadn't seen another vehicle since they left the interstate. "We're here."

Fields of withered cornstalks lined the bumpy track on either side. Joseph spotted a few trees up ahead, and glimpsed a house beyond. "Careful, pard," he said.

"I see it." George slowed the truck until they were creeping along.

The light was turning golden as they cleared the trees. A two-story farmhouse sat to one side of the track, barn and outbuildings to the other side, and a corral beyond, all in a state of extreme disrepair. The place looked as if it had been abandoned for years.

The men exchanged looks. "We should leave," George said.

"We should," Joseph said, tamping down his fear. "But I need to have it out with that thing."

"Wouldn't it be better to do it on your own turf?"

Joseph swung the door open. "This *is* my turf, pard," he said with a bravado he didn't feel. "As of right now." He stepped down and slammed the truck door. Then he walked up to the house, yelling, "Hello! Anybody home? Dolores?" He heard George shut the driver's side door and begin muttering to himself. He risked a glance back; George was unloading the bits and pieces of their snare from the truck bed: a tarp with weights tied to the corners, a coil of rope, and some miscellaneous tools.

It struck Joseph how ill-prepared they were. He nearly ran back to the truck. Instead, "Hello?" he called again. "Hey, Dolores! We're here! Where are you? Where's your brother?"

"He'll be along," a sultry voice said beside him.

Joseph turned, startled, to find the woman standing within arm's reach. "There you are," he said, knowing it sounded lame. He tried to recover by sweeping an arm out at the general decay. "I thought you told George he lived here."

"He does." She smiled, revealing very white, very pointy teeth. Apparently they hadn't been part of the costume. "So do I. Want to see?"

Joseph blinked. Had she just come on to him? "Maybe later," he hedged. "After we've wrapped up your little problem for you. Where have you been finding the dead livestock? That would probably be a good place to start."

She pouted briefly, then gave him a sly smile. "In the barn," she said. "This way."

Joseph followed, his steps lagging.

As she passed George, she beckoned with a clawlike fingernail. "You come, too."

George traded a look with Joseph as he fell into step beside him. "Did you see where she came from?" Joseph asked in a whisper.

"No," George said quietly. "I looked up and she was standing next to you."

Joseph thought for a second. "I want you to get back in the truck and get out of here."

"And leave you behind? Not a chance, pard. Looks Far would kill me."

"I can take care of myself, but it'll be easier if I'm not trying to save *you*," Joseph hissed. It was too late now, anyway, he realized; Dolores had pulled open the sagging barn door and was waiting for them. He cursed under his breath and told George, "Stay by the door." Then he followed the woman into the barn.

He blinked as his eyes adjusted to the gloom. The interior of the barn had the same abandoned air as the rest of the place. "Okay," he said, feeling anger rising, as she turned to face him. "Let's cut to the chase, shall we? There's no livestock. You set me up so you could fight me. That's why you tracked me down the other night, isn't it? To fight me? To battle to the death, for honor and glory?"

"I don't *want* to fight you," she purred. "We can do this nice and easy." She began walking toward him.

As she approached, he felt Coyote awaken inside him. He grinned fiercely to himself. This woman might think she knew what he was capable of, but she didn't know he had a Trickster God on his side. *Oh, sweetheart. You ain't seen nothing yet.*

"I bet you don't even have a brother," he went on, letting Coyote begin to take over.

She laughed. "Say hello, Miguel," she said, looking over Joseph's shoulder. He stepped to one side and looked back toward the door – where a chupacabra held George with one scaly forearm across his throat. George's eyes bulged with fear.

"Let him go," Joseph said quietly. "I'll give you what you want, but let him go. He's of no use to you."

"Oh, but he is," Dolores said. "He is our insurance that you will cooperate."

Cooperate? "I don't want to fight you"? What the hell? "Look," he said, "what is this all about?"

Her eyes glowed blood-red. "Our kind were never very numerous. Now, we are fewer every year. We must improve our bloodline in order to survive. And you have a certain…flexibility…we lack." She gave him a sultry smile.

Joseph's eyes widened as her meaning dawned on him. "You want to *sleep* with me?"

"We need your versatility. Miguel said you put on quite a show the other evening."

Joseph glanced again at the monster holding George. The creature seemed to be grinning at him.

Mentally, he threw up his hands. *Go for it,* he told the god, surrendering control. *This is more your kind of thing, anyway.*

Gleefully, Coyote complied. "Well," He said, shaking Joseph's head, "I'm flattered, but I don't date outside My species." Then He whipped off Joseph's clothes and shifted into as close an approximation of a chupacabra as He could manage. "There. That's better," He growled.

The woman's face registered shocked delight. Then she, too, shifted. In the blink of an eye, she was a slightly smaller version of her brother. She bounded toward him on all fours and presented her backside to him.

Oh, this is too easy. A split second later, Joseph Coyote had become Joseph Grizzly, and Dolores was flat on the ground under Him. She screeched, flailing her limbs, as He held her in place with a single massive paw. Her brother roared, clenching George's windpipe tighter.

"If you want your sister to live," He growled, "let My friend go."

With another roar, the male chupacabra released George and came at Him fast.

Joseph took back control, and made sure George was out of the way before he shifted again. Miguel grabbed at the air where the bear had been; then he grabbed futilely at the boa constrictor that had wrapped itself around his chest. Dolores was on her feet by then; still screeching, she began pounding on the snake, trying to get it to let go. Then she took a step back and unsheathed two claws on her right forepaw, which she tried to jam through the boa constrictor's scaly hide. In response, Joseph Boa uncoiled his tail, threw it around her hand, and tightened it until he felt the bones crack. He released her just as Miguel lost consciousness and dropped to the floor.

"You killed him!" Dolores shrieked, cradling her now-useless hand. She was back in human form. Miguel, too, had shifted as he fell; a dark-haired youth, who looked all of fourteen, now lay on the dirt floor of the ruined barn.

"He's not dead," Joseph said, willing it to be true, as he bent to pick up his clothes. But a vicious boot toe connected with his chin; he flew backward and landed against the post of a horse stall, seeing stars.

"You killed my baby brother!" she shrieked now, shaking the boy. "You – you *monster!*"

And the pot calls the kettle black. "I might have cracked one of his ribs," he admitted. "Or two."

Dolores turned to him, her face distorted with rage. "He has stopped breathing. I will *kill* you for this!" She shifted again and threw herself at Joseph.

Ah, shit. I didn't mean to kill him. Cursing himself for his carelessness, he became a pigeon and flew up to the rafters, well out of her reach. He shifted back and straddled the crossbeam, hoping he didn't end up with a splinter in an unfortunate place.

She screamed her frustration for several minutes. Joseph let her get it out of her system. Then, when she seemed to be winding down, he said, "Look, Dolores. We can keep doing this over and over again, but I'm always going to be able to escape."

She sat in the dirt next to her brother, cradling her broken hand and weeping.

"How did you find out about me, anyway?" Joseph asked.

"We could *smell* you," she said harshly. "As soon as we got near Denver, we smelled skinwalker. You were easy to track – you never think to hide your scent."

"And yet you decided I'd make a terrific father."

"We wanted your seed only." She spat. "Now I would not even take that."

"Good," Joseph said, "because you're not getting it."

That brought on a fresh bout of weeping. Joseph waited with his arms crossed, shivering now and then. The temperature was dropping as night came on. He glanced out the open barn door; golden hour was over and dusk was falling fast. Very soon, he was either going to have to get down and get dressed, or shift into something furry, if he didn't want to risk hypothermia.

Then he heard sirens, and rolled his eyes. *Thanks a lot, George. Thanks one hell of a lot. Now I've got a dead body to explain to the cops.*

Dolores heard the sirens, too. She stopped crying and raised her head in a panic, looking toward the barn door.

Joseph took the opening. Shifting into an owl, he glided to the floor on silent wings. Then, human again, he picked up a rusty horseshoe and used it to knock Dolores flat. As he quickly donned his clothes, he spared a glance for the two chupacabras lying side by side on the barn floor. Then he blinked and stared, as Miguel's body dematerialized before his eyes. In a moment, there was nothing but a damp spot in the dirt next to Dolores.

He checked to make sure she was still breathing. Then he stepped outside and, exhausted by all the shifting he'd just done, slumped against the wall of the barn to wait for the cavalry.

The county deputy was dubious of their story. Joseph didn't blame him, even as he spun it up with as earnest a face as he could manage: "We met her at a party in Denver the other night. She lured us out here to do some repairs for her. Said she was an heiress and she'd pay us twenty thousand dollars to get the house back in livable shape. Well, we got out here and found it like this, and when we told her she ought to tear the whole thing down and start over, she went crazy on us."

"And attacked you with the horseshoe." The deputy was writing it all down, but it was clear he wasn't buying it.

"Right. So I wrestled it away from her and whacked her on the head with it."

The deputy looked up at him. "And how'd her hand get crushed, again?"

"I told you," Joseph said patiently. "She got it caught in the truck door while George was getting away."

George nodded in corroboration.

The deputy sighed and shut his notebook. "All right. You two are free to go for now. We may call you with more questions later."

George and Joseph thanked him and shook his hand. Then they got in the truck, maneuvered it around the ambulance into which the paramedics were still loading Dolores, and hightailed it home.

"I'm surprised they let us go," George said, once they were well across the county line. "They could have booked you for assault."

Joseph gave a crooked grin. "Yeah. It would have been better for our story if one of us had been hurt." His smile faded. "They still might, you know. Depending on what she says when she comes to."

"Maybe not," George said. "It's our word against hers. They may just drop the whole thing. What happened to Miguel, anyway?"

Joseph's guilt came back in a rush. "I turned into a boa constrictor and squeezed him to death," he said miserably.

"Jesus."

"I didn't mean to kill him. I just wanted to knock him out."

"Where'd his body go?"

"It…dissolved." Joseph saw the image in his mind again, and shuddered. "Pretty gruesome to watch."

"I bet it was," George said, his face lit by the glow of the truck's instrument panel. "Good thing, though, huh? You'd be facing a murder rap otherwise."

Joseph nodded and sighed. They were quiet for several miles, during which Joseph sent a silent appeal to the gods to lead Miguel home. Then he leaned his head against the door and fell into a doze.

He woke up fast when George said, "So about that shifting thing you do."

Joseph felt his face grow warm. "You saw it, didn't you?"

"I did. And…." George cleared his throat. "And while I knew you could do it, because I've seen the end result numerous times, I'd never seen you actually do it before." He paused. Joseph dreaded his next words, but all he said was, "It's quite a talent."

Joseph snorted. "That's one way to put it." He waited out another pause, his anxiety increasing with each passing second. Finally, he said, "I can find another place to live."

"Oh, hell, Joseph. That's not why I brought it up."

He breathed a bit easier. But still he asked, "Then why *did* you bring it up?"

George fiddled with the heater for a second. "It'll just take some getting used to, is all. The reality of it, I mean. For me."

Joseph nodded. The rest of the trip passed in silence, until they pulled into the driveway. Then Joseph turned to his friend and said, "It's not over, you know. With her."

"I know." George shut off the truck. "But she's not coming back tonight. And I don't know about you, but I'm dead on my feet. Let's get some sleep."

Joseph slept the deep, dreamless sleep of the exhausted shapeshifter. But the situation must have been percolating in his mind all night, because a new thought occurred to him as soon as he awoke.

"I need to help her," he told George as they sat down to breakfast.

George paused in the act of putting a forkful of eggs into his mouth. "No, you don't." He ate the eggs, made a face, and reached for the bottle of hot sauce. "That's just your guilt talking."

"Maybe," Joseph allowed. "But now she's alone, and it's my fault. And I know what it feels like to be one of a kind."

George put down his fork. "Look, Drama Boy. She's alone because she and her brother dreamed up some cockamamie scheme to get you to have sex with her, and it backfired on them. Okay? You don't need to play do-gooder. She got what she deserved. Are you gonna eat those eggs?"

Wordlessly, he handed his plate over to George. Maybe he *was* being dramatic, he thought. *But she's not going to go away. I need to either help her, or kill her. And I'm tired of killing.*

Late that night, a great horned owl flew silently across the plains. Careless night creatures caught his eye as he flew, but his goal wasn't dinner.

He landed on the ground outside a hospital building, then shrunk to the size and shape of a field mouse. Clambering up a drainpipe, he found a crevice big enough to squeeze into. Soon he was scooting into a closet.

A few minutes later, a tall, ponytailed man in scrubs walked out of the closet. He grabbed a stethoscope from an unattended desk and hung it around his neck as if he knew what to do with it. Then he made his way briskly to Dolores's room. He glanced over the chart on her door, noting the word "combative." *Great. Just great.* Taking a deep breath, he walked in as quietly as he could and pulled the door shut behind him.

She was asleep – sedated, he assumed. Her broken hand was set in plaster; her hair was shaved where he'd clocked her with the horseshoe and a bandage covered the wound. He found himself awash in an odd mixture of tenderness and guilt. Gently, he shook her undamaged shoulder. "Dolores," he murmured. "Wake up. We need to talk."

Her eyes fluttered open. Then she leaped from the bed, tearing the IV out of her hand. The flimsy stand clattered and tipped over onto the bed as she backed into a corner. "You," she breathed.

"Don't make so much racket," he said, casting a worried glance at the closed door. "I only want to talk to you."

"You killed my brother!" she shrieked.

"And I want to apologize for that," Joseph began, pushing at her with both hands. "Keep your voice down." He glanced back again at the door. When he turned back, he was looking at the chupacabra.

Her leathery skin was a delicate blue, but that was the only girly thing about her. Her hands had become claws with three razor-sharp tips apiece. The cast that had been formed to her human right hand now dangled, split asunder, from her forepaw. Her pointy teeth gleamed as she roared. Then she lunged for him.

He dodged her, trying to keep the bed between them. But she cleared it in one bound, knocking it askew, the braked wheels scraping the tile floor. The tray table went down, dumping water from the plastic pitcher it had held. Joseph slipped in it and did an inadvertent somersault across the bed, fetching up against the wall in the far corner.

The door opened, and a frowning orderly poked his head in. Then he paled. "What the hell is that?" he yelled to Joseph.

"I don't know, man," Joseph yelled back as he struggled to his feet. "I came in to take the patient's vitals and found this thing!"

Dolores roared and went for Joseph again.

"Security!" the man at the door yelled. "Room 223, stat!" He slammed the door and ran.

Terrific. Thanks a lot, pal. Joseph dodged her yet again, then tried to maneuver her into a corner so he could push the bed up against her. He thought that might hold her for a few moments. But she was wise to him. She shoved the bed against the door, leaving a clear path between her and Joseph. Hissing in pleasure, she leaped.

He shifted.

She landed on an empty pile of scrubs, coming down hard on her injured forepaw. She shrieked in pain and fury.

Joseph Fly lit on the ceiling and watched the rest of the scene upside-down. The orderly came back with a security guard, and together they pushed their way into the room. The guard was clearly out of his league; he drew his pistol and yelled, "Put your hands up!"

Dolores roared. She tried to leap toward the guard from a crouch, but one of her feet slipped on the wet floor and she went sideways. If she hadn't, the guard might only have winged her with his shot. Instead, she took the bullet in the eye. Joseph was sure she was dead before she hit the ground.

"What the hell...?" the orderly said as the monster resumed Dolores's shape. Blood wept from her ruined eye.

"Is that your missing patient?" the guard asked.

"Yeah," the orderly said. "Yeah, it is."

"But it was a monster, right?" the guard said. "I mean, we both saw it." Joseph felt for the guy. He'd been in the same situation just the day before.

"Yeah, it was," the orderly said again. "Hey, I wonder what happened to the other orderly. The guy who was in here with her." He skirted the dead woman and picked up the scrubs and stethoscope. "Did he leave naked?"

"Oh, my God," the guard said. "Would you look at that." The orderly turned, and Joseph watched both of them stare bug-eyed at Dolores's dissolving corpse. The spent bullet made a *tink* as it hit the floor where her head had been.

They stared at one another for a few moments. Then the orderly said, "I think the patient checked herself out."

"I'm good with that," said the guard as he holstered his weapon. He sounded relieved. "Why don't you straighten up in here?"

"Yeah. I'll get a mop." The two of them spent another minute or two just looking at each other. Then the guard shook his head slightly and bent to retrieve the bullet. When the men finally opened the door, Joseph Fly buzzed out behind them.

"You look chipper this morning," George said as a bleary-eyed Joseph poured himself a second cup of coffee.

"Didn't sleep well," he mumbled.

"Still think you need to go and help Dolores, huh?"

Joseph winced at her name. "Too late. She's dead."

George motioned his friend to sit down. "What happened, pard?" he asked gently.

Joseph told him.

At the end of it, George sat back and said, "Well, I know you're not gonna agree with me, but I still think she got what she deserved."

Joseph took a sip of his coffee, grimaced, and poured it down the sink. Then he sighed. "I know. I just…. She was one of a kind, George."

"She was."

"Is that the only good end for a creature like her?" He felt as if he were pleading with his friend. "Do we have to kill them? Is that the only answer?"

"It's the only answer for the crazy ones," George said. "But you're not crazy."

Joseph could feel Coyote grinning somewhere inside him. He huffed a laugh. "Some days," he said, "I wonder."

A Weekend Away

I try to avoid overworked cliches, which is why you won't see many *flavor-of-the-month monsters in my books. For example, I write about shapeshifters, but none of them are werewolves. However, for* 13 Bites Vol. III, *which was published in the fall of 2015, I broke my own rule and wrote a zombie story.*

"Man, I can't wait to get to the beach," Albert said as he and Grier motored along the two-lane highway. "I've had such a rotten week. All I could think about was getting away at the end of it. With you." He reached across the console of his SUV and squeezed her hand.

Grier gave him a smile and settled back in her seat. "It's been more like a rotten month for me." She closed her eyes, willing away mental images of the big moment several days before, when it had all come down. "I don't want to think about any of that. I just want to lie in the sun and listen to the waves." She threw a glance at the man behind the wheel and added belatedly, "With you."

He gave her a grin that was almost a leer. "I hope we'll do more than just lie in the sun."

Grier winked at him and closed her eyes again. If she didn't look at the road, she wouldn't be tempted to wrench the steering wheel out of his hands. Albert was a perfectly competent driver; there was nothing wrong with letting someone else take charge, every now and then. And wasn't that the reason she had agreed to this trip? To hand over command for a little while?

She opened her eyes a tiny bit and regarded Albert through her lashes. She didn't know him very well. They had met in a bar during the run-up to her most recent work-related crisis. She didn't usually go to bars, but she'd needed desperately to unwind that night, amongst people who didn't know anything about what she did for a living. Albert had chatted her up almost immediately. He was a sales rep for a vacuum cleaner company, in town on one of his regular swings through the area. One drink had led to another, and she'd ended up easing some of her edginess in his hotel room. She had expected it to be a one-night stand, but then he texted her with an invitation to this out-of-the-way spot. When her project wrapped up with a bang the next day, she took it as a sign.

"I can't believe I found such a great deal on this place," he said. "Just think of it, Grier – we'll have a whole island to ourselves. And in their busy season, too."

"Maybe there's something wrong with the place," she murmured.

"The reviewers didn't think so," he said. "Although there weren't any reviews from the last few months. Maybe the cottage has been under renovation or something."

"Maybe," she echoed. She felt a slight bump as the tires went over something in the road – an expansion joint, she assumed – and immediately, the road they traveled on sounded different. Like a bridge or a causeway. She opened her eyes all the way and discovered she was right: they were traversing a long causeway over open water, with nothing at the end but a knot of sand and trees.

"There it is," Albert said unnecessarily, pointing straight ahead. "Racek Island. Our home for the next two nights and three days." He grinned at her again.

Grier couldn't help herself; her training kicked in. She scanned the island for escape routes as she asked, "Is this the only way to the island from the mainland?"

"I think there's a marina."

"But no ferry service? What about a landing field?"

He gave her a surprised look. "You want to leave already? We're not even there yet!"

She laughed self-consciously. "Sorry. I'm a little claustrophobic. I like to know my exit routes."

They both fell silent as their destination grew larger before them. No one else was on the causeway. Grier's unease grew as she realized she hadn't seen another vehicle since they'd left the highway.

Albert slowed the SUV to a stop. "I can turn around, if you want."

"No, I want to go," she said quickly. "Don't mind me – I'm just quirky." *And this is just the sort of thinking I'm here to escape from.*

"You're sure?"

She plastered a smile on her face. "Of course I'm sure. Keep driving."

He sighed. "Okay," he said, and they were moving again.

Upon exiting the causeway, they turned left – the only way they could go – and followed the bumpy asphalt road around the dune-swept island. Grier saw no marina, no landing strip, and no other sign of life – just a copse of trees in the middle of the island. There was also no cell phone service, but she had expected that.

"This must be the place," said Albert as he stopped in front of the only habitation they had seen: a rambling beach cottage that faced the glittering water, its back to the tiny forest.

"I think I've figured out why it was so cheap," said Grier, examining the place through the windshield. The weathered siding and sand-drifted path to the porch spoke of neglect.

Albert shrugged. "The interior shots online looked really nice. Come on." He was already half out of the car. "If it's terrible, we'll leave."

She nodded, but still couldn't bring herself to open the door. "Could we back in?" she asked.

He laughed and shook his head. "If it'll help your claustrophobia, sure. Anything." He swung back inside and fired up the engine, then parked nose out and perpendicular to the road. "Better?"

"Yes, thanks," she said with a small sigh of relief.

At the back of the truck, Albert handed her grocery bags and her suitcase. She took three steps away from the truck and stopped dead, the back of her neck prickling. It felt as if a thousand eyes were on her, watching her, weighing her worth as an adversary.

Albert's hand on her shoulder made her jump. "Are you okay?" he asked. "Sorry. I didn't mean to startle you."

She laughed a little again. "Yeah, I'm fine. It's crazy, I know, but for a minute I thought someone was watching me."

His hand caressed her arm as he pressed himself against her. "That was me," he whispered in her ear.

She turned her head and let him kiss her. "Let's go in," he said, when they came up for air.

The interior was lovely. So was the bed.

A little while later, they found their swimsuits. "Do we even need these?" Albert asked, holding his up with one finger. "It's not like there's anybody else on the island."

Grier tried to shrug as she fastened her bikini top. "Boaters might pass by."

"I guess you're right," he said, eyeing her up and down. "Better to keep that view all to myself."

She threw him a come-hither look as she picked up the blanket and sunscreen. As she walked through the living room to the kitchen for the wine, she looked briefly at her leather handbag, which she'd tossed onto the sofa in her haste to get inside. She could bring it. She might need the weapon concealed inside.

As soon as that thought occurred to her, she chided herself for being silly. Albert was right – they were alone. And she had come here to relax and get away from the paranoia. She forced herself not to look at the bag as she headed for the door.

Three steps away from the cottage, she shuddered. She was being watched – she was sure of it. And the watcher was concealed in the grove of trees.

She groaned and shook her head. "No," she said aloud. "I need this vacation." She refused to let paranoia ruin it for her. Resolutely, she crossed the road and headed for the water.

Albert was waiting for her with an ice bucket and glasses. She spread out the blanket while he iced down the wine. Then they took a little extra time putting sunscreen on each other. Somehow her bikini top got misplaced, but she found she didn't care.

A few moments later, she heard Albert snoring softly. She shook her head and walked down to the water.

The water was warm and almost as calm as a swimming pool. Grier swam out a short distance, then leaned back and let her mind drift. Her breathing slowed. She was so relaxed that she almost fell asleep.

Something small and almost weightless touched her belly. She opened her eyes and beheld a seagull, standing on her as if she were a piling at a pier. "Go away," she said. "Shoo." She splashed it with one hand.

But the bird didn't shoo. It regarded her with red-rimmed, dead-looking eyes.

"Aw, shit," Grier said, memories of the past week flooding back. "Not here, too!"

At that moment, Albert screamed. "Shit," she said again, and executed a twisting, convulsive dive to dislodge the gull. Then she swam back to shore with everything she had.

The gull followed her, its dead wings shedding feathers as it flew. The feathers reminded her of shredded pillows, which reminded her of the hotel room where it had all come down. *Rats. Rats! With dead little eyes and tiny bloodied muzzles, ripping through everything in their way to get to me...and then the boom as the team kicked open the door...* She took a deep breath and looked toward the shoreline. Albert wasn't in sight – she hoped he had made it to the cottage intact and was now packing their stuff – but a welcoming committee awaited her at the waterline: a string of blue crabs, waving their pincers in the air as if to say hello. Tattered gulls wheeled overhead.

And now she saw what had been watching her in the woods: deer. Three of them were lined up next to the cottage, all with mangy fur and eyes deader than a mounted trophy head.

She treaded water for a few moments, weighing her options. Zombies can't move any faster than their living versions can, so she judged she could make an end-run around the crabs. The birds would be tougher to out-maneuver, but losing their flight feathers was taking a toll on their speed and mobility. She glanced back on her next breath to find her original avian companion; he or she had fallen behind and seemed to be having trouble staying in the air.

The big problem was going to be the deer. They could block her access to the cottage. Where she'd left her weapon. Which her gut instinct had told her not to do.

She hoped Albert had had the sense to get inside the cottage – although his smartest move would have been to get back in the SUV and get out. She was grateful he hadn't. It meant they might both still survive.

"Shit," she repeated as her knees hit sand. It was now or never.

She crouched in the shallows, digging her toes in for traction, but the sand under her feet dribbled away. She sighed, then sucked in a breath and took off at a run anyway, veering wide to the right to avoid the crabs. She was right – they couldn't skitter toward her that fast. And while the gulls made a lot of moaning noises, they were flying erratically, knocking into each other and dislodging more feathers and even an occasional wing. The disabled gulls flopped around on the beach, but most quickly got their feet under them and followed after the crabs in a sort of shambling strut.

Grier noted all of this in a flash before she reached the road. Then she turned toward the cottage door. Just as she had expected, the deer were on an intercept course. She crossed the road and stopped. "Albert!" she cried, hoping he was inside the house.

No response.

She scuttled to the far side of the SUV to check whether he was inside the vehicle. He wasn't, and of course the doors were locked. Mentally cursing city dwellers and their habitual ways, she called out again, "Albert! Are you inside? Answer me!"

He looked through the window next to the door, wearing a dazed look.

"Thank God you're all right," she called. "Throw me my purse!"

"Why?" he called in a trembling voice. "What if you're one of them?"

She rolled her eyes. "I'm talking, aren't I?"

"Yeah."

"So I can't be one of them. They can't talk." She glanced toward the beach; the crabs had reached the far edge of the asphalt. "Look, we don't have time for this. I can get us out alive, but you have to do what I what I say. Throw me my purse!"

"Why?" That sounded less horrified and more insulted that she was trying to boss him around.

Losing all patience, she yelled, "Because I'm a zombie hunter and my gun is inside it!"

Silence ensued, during which Grier noticed the deer heading to her side of the SUV. On the beach side, the crabs were nearly across the road. Her window of opportunity was about to close. "Screw it," she muttered, and sprinted around the front of the vehicle toward the cottage.

That door, too, was locked. She pounded on it in frustration, and a moment later, she heard the lock snick open. "Sorry," said Albert as he opened the door. "I didn't want them to come in."

"They couldn't have gotten in anyway," she said, heading immediately for her bag. "They can't work the doorknob. None of them have opposable thumbs." Yes, her service weapon was still there. She took it with her into the bedroom to change.

"Oh," he said, following her. "I didn't think of that. What are you doing?"

Fastening her bra in the back, she said, "Getting dressed. We're leaving." She pulled a t-shirt over her head and knotted it under her breasts.

"What about the blanket and the wine? I left everything on the beach."

She was about to snap at him about not going back for it now, when she took a good look at him and changed her mind. His face was pale, his forehead damp. "Albert," she said gently, "what happened to you?"

"One of them bit me," he said, his voice trembling as he pointed down at his bloody big toe. "I'm going to be one of them, aren't I? I'm going to be a zombie!"

Probably. "No," she said firmly. "The virus doesn't jump species."

"Are you sure?"

"Not from crab to human."

He looked down at his toe. "It might have been a seagull."

That's more problematic. "I haven't heard of that happening, either," she lied as her heart sank. "But we need to get you to a hospital, in any case. Let's get dressed and get in the truck. I'll drive."

"Okay," he said, and began to pull his trousers on, his toe leaving bloody smears on the carpet.

So much for letting someone else take control for a few days. She finished dressing, re-packed for both of them, and led him to the door. "Stay here," she said, and looked outside to see where things stood.

The crabs, the bedraggled gulls, and the deer all stood between them and the truck. She sighed. "This isn't going to be pretty," she said. "Stay low and don't come out until I say it's okay." He nodded, and she stepped out onto the porch.

Her semi-automatic zombie-killer special made quick work of the deer and the gulls. The crabs were tougher – their shells made for a fairly strong shield against her bullets, and their brains were a smaller target. But in the end, she got them all. "Okay," she called to Albert, shoving her weapon into the waistband of her jeans. "You can come out now."

No answer. She went back in the cottage and found him slumped on the floor next to the suitcases. "Well, that's just great," she muttered, slinging him over a shoulder. She knew it meant it was probably already too late to save him, but she intended to try anyway.

She was grateful to discover that she wouldn't have to go through his pockets; he had been holding the SUV keys when he fell. She pushed the unlocking button on the remote and picked her way through the gore and tiny bodies to the vehicle. There, she manhandled him across the back seat, belting him in for good measure. Then she went back inside to get the luggage.

When she came back out, her old friend the gull was waiting for her on the porch. It must have feasted on blown-out brains on its way in; its beak dripped with gore.

"Nice to see you again," she said as she set down a suitcase and pulled out her gun. It tried to take flight, but it was still floundering to launch itself when she blew its head away.

Grier lost no time packing the car and firing up the engine. With a roar, she fishtailed out of the parking space and got out of there as fast as the crumbling asphalt track would allow. She half expected to find zombie fish and crustaceans barricading the causeway, but when she got there, she found nothing between her and the mainland. Gratefully, she hit the gas.

As soon as she reached the highway, she called in to work. "Dispatch," said a familiar voice on the other end of the line. Angie was working another double-shift. They needed to get more help, and fast, or exhaustion would kill them all before the zombies could.

"Lieutenant Marshall, reporting an infestation on Racek Island," she said crisply. "Infected species include seagulls, blue crabs, and deer. Situation mitigated, but mop-up team advised."

"Grier?" said a different and no less familiar voice – that of Captain Polk, her superior officer. "I thought I told you to take a few days off."

"You did, sir."

"Well, get back in here. We have a crisis on our hands."

"Crisis, sir?" She muted the phone as Albert began moaning in the back seat. Quick as lightning, she pulled her gun out of her bag and shot him in the face.

For a moment, she couldn't hear anything; the noise in such an enclosed space had temporarily deafened her. As her hearing cleared, "...Henderson," was all she could make out.

As brains and blood dripped from the ceiling of the SUV, Grier unmuted the phone. "Say again, sir?"

"I said, Hendricks is one of them!" Polk nearly shouted. Then, more subdued, "A rat bit her on her way in to work this morning."

"This morning...?" said Grier. "I don't understand. She was vaccinated the same day I was."

"The virus mutated," Polk told her. "Hendricks isn't the first fatality we've heard about." His tone gentled. "Sorry. I know you two were close."

Were close. Grier knew what that meant: all that was left of Sallie was a pile of ash.

"What's your E.T.A.?" Polk asked.

"Half an hour."

"Good. Be careful, Grier."

She nodded and ended the call, her index finger smearing Albert's blood across the face of her phone. She realized her hair was covered in blood and diseased tissue, but she had no time to stop to clean it off. She would have to use the decontamination facility at headquarters, after dodging who-knew-what in the shadows to get in the door.

She and Sallie Hendricks had gone through training together. Always had each other's backs. Sallie had been first through the hotel doorway when it all went down. They'd joked later about her being Grier's rat cavalry, and that next time it would be Grier's turn.

But Grier hadn't been there when Sallie needed her, and now she'd never get the chance.

Grier's lower lip began to quiver, but she banished it. No time to mourn. She had to get to work.

Half an hour later, she pulled up to the side door of the agency and got out of the SUV. She stumbled as her feet hit the pavement, surprising her. She supposed her feet had gone numb on the long drive.

As the door guard approached, she flashed her ID and said, "Hello, soldier. Call the hazmat crew to clean this up. I need to get inside to talk to Captain Polk." She started to walk past him, but he stepped into her path.

"Lieutenant?" the guard asked with a frown. "Are you feeling all right?"

"I'm fine," she said. Or tried to say. She realized her lips weren't forming words.

He pointed to her bare torso. "What's that?"

She looked down at the mean-looking red welt that had formed on her belly. "That damned seagull," she said, but it came out as a moan.

Then the guard was on his radio, and a white-suited hazmat team came rushing out to meet her.

Her last conscious thought in the incinerator bag, as the knockout gas began rushing in through the red hose, was that she had achieved what she'd set out to do that weekend, after all. At last, someone else would have to be in charge.

Intercept

As I said in the Introduction, Indies Unlimited holds a flash fiction contest every week. The administrators supply a photo and a prompt (this year, it's only a photo), and authors are invited to use them as the basis for writing a 250-word story. Each week's winning story is published in an anthology at the end of the year. The following story was published, in a slightly different form, in the Indies Unlimited 2013 Flash Fiction Anthology. *For this collection, I've rewritten the beginning of the story to include details from the prompt.*

We could see the thing on the horizon – even though the radar screen in front of me still claimed nothing was there.

We had passengers aboard – survivors of ships that had encountered whatever it was – and we had found their stories were hard to swallow. But the reality was worse. Much worse.

When I looked again at the horizon, I realized we weren't moving to intercept the unknown craft so much as *it* was moving to intercept *us*. We were in the middle of the Chesapeake Bay, nowhere near Bermuda. How could this be happening?

But it was. Every time I looked at the thing, it was closer. It had to be moving impossibly fast.

Finally the captain sprang to life. "Battle stations!" he roared.

I focused on the useless radar screens before me as the klaxons began wailing.

"Radar! Report!" Cappy barked at me.

I shrugged. "Still nothing, sir."

"Should we turn, sir?" asked Klein at the helm.

Cappy's shoulders sagged. Then, resolutely, he lifted them again. "No," he said. "Hold your course."

One of the survivors burst through the bridge door. "Hard about!" he shrieked, eyes wide as a madman's, as he grabbed Cappy's shoulders and shook him. Another sailor and I sprang from our seats to peel him off.

"No," Cappy said again. "We won't turn tail and run."

The man collapsed and curled into a ball, keening.

I turned back to the window. The thing was almost on us. It was bigger than an aircraft carrier, its hide a sickly, pulsing green. And its eyes –

Cappy grabbed the microphone, bellowing, "This is the U.S. Coast Guard cutter Intrepid. State your name and affiliation."

The leviathan blinked. Then, with a roar, it opened its maw and…bit.

When I came to, I was clinging to a piece of wreckage. I saw no one else – except the survivor who had tried to save us. "Hard about," he muttered as he began to sob. "Hard about!"

Our Monsters Are More Subtle

While we're still at sea, I'll let you judge whether a wendigo is more subtle than a leviathan that snacks on Coast Guard cutters. This story is part of the Land, Sea, Sky trilogy. It happens not long after the events in Scorched Earth and it's set not too far from where I grew up. I've published the story at Wattpad.

Note: The line Whitaker sings is from "The Wendigo" by Algernon Blackwood, published in 1910 and available online here: http://www.gutenberg.org/files/10897/10897-h/10897-h.htm

"It's good to be home," Darrell murmured. Bare toes sunk deep in the cold New Buffalo sand, he watched the waves as they scudded across Lake Michigan, the whitecaps glowing pink in the early morning light. Steam wafted from the top of the power company's cooling tower at Michigan City. Chicago – where he and his fiancée, Tess, had seen their friends Sue and Robbie married earlier in the week – was a smudge on the western horizon.

It was shaping up to be another beautiful October day. He turned to the east, raised his hands to the sky, and began to chant a greeting to the sun in his native Potawatomi.

He was only partway through the chant when an unfamiliar voice called out, "Good morning!" His concentration broken, Darrell sighed and turned to see who had interrupted him.

A man in khakis and an expensive-looking winter jacket picked his way down the sand-swamped stairs between the beach and the road. Darrell thought he looked like one of the summer people – the local term for Chicago residents who owned cottages on the Indiana and Michigan side of the lake. He returned the greeting politely and waited for the man to catch up to him.

"New here?" the man asked as he stuck out his hand. The wind off the lake played havoc with his carefully-groomed dark hair.

Darrell shook hands. "Old here, actually. Darrell Warren." He watched the man's face for a reaction; he'd received a fair amount of press after the ayalendo incident a couple of years before, although not as much as Tess got on a regular basis via her network news job. But his name clearly didn't ring a bell with the stranger. He went on, "I grew up in Dowagiac. We're just back for a visit."

"Ah. I wondered why I hadn't seen you around before. I'm Graham Whitaker. I'm looking at some places in Forest Beach."

"The old YMCA summer camp." Darrell nodded. "I wasn't even a twinkle in my father's eye when they sold the place, back in the 1980s. But people were still upset about it when I was a kid – pristine woods and dunes, all bulldozed under for multi-million-dollar homes."

Whitaker squinted at him against the wind. "There's always somebody who complains about progress. And anyway, that was almost fifty years ago. Ancient history."

"I suppose that's true," Darrell conceded, fighting a sudden urge to flee. Whitaker gave off an odd vibe that he couldn't quite put his finger on.

"Yep," the man went on. "And those houses are showing their age now. So much potential here." As Whitaker turned his gaze inland, Darrell could see a hungry glint in his eye. He shuddered and backed off a step, but the man didn't appear to notice. A moment more, and Whitaker recalled himself. "Well. Nice to meet you." He fished in his pants pocket for a moment, brought out a business card holder, and extracted a card, which he handed to Darrell. Darrell pocketed the card without a glance as he pulled his own card holder from the back pocket of his jeans and completed the ritual exchange.

Whitaker frowned as he studied Darrell's card. "Navy man, huh?" was all he said.

"Yes, sir." Darrell suppressed a grin. His cards were a masterpiece of obfuscation, if he did say so himself. The alphabet soup he'd invented for the name of his command was designed to be impressive without giving away anything of its clandestine nature.

"Hope to run into you again soon," Whitaker said, and turned back to the stairs.

Darrell felt his shoulders relax as the man got farther away. He wondered at that. And as he heard Whitaker's car pull away, he wondered why the man would stop just to say hello.

Shrugging, he turned back to the rising sun to finish his prayer. Then he donned his shoes, mounted the stairs himself, and – with a last look back at the glittering water – began the two-block walk to his and Tess's rented condo.

He let himself in quietly. As he expected, Tess was still in bed, but she sat up as he entered the bedroom. "Jesus," she said, her eyes still shut, "what's that smell?"

He stopped just inside the door. "What smell?"

"Augh." She wrinkled her nose and fanned a hand in front of her face. "Smells like you've been rolling in dead things."

Only then did he pull out Whitaker's card to read it:

Lakefront Associates
Developers
Graham R. Whitaker, Partner

Remembering the hungry look in Whitaker's eye, Darrell said, "Maybe I have."

"I've met him," Gus said. The old Potawatomi medicine man, Darrell's mentor back when he'd trained as a *midew*, sat forward in his recliner and took the mug of tea Tess handed him. "He's been sniffing around here, looking to buy up some of the tribe's land."

"He can't," Darrell said, surprised.

Gus nodded as he took a sip. "Ah. That hits the spot. Thank you, daughter."

"It's just tea," Tess said. She seemed a little in awe of the old man. Darrell wrapped an arm around her shoulders and kissed the top of her head before taking a sip from his own mug.

"You're right," Gus said to Darrell. "The tribe can't sell land it doesn't own, no matter what these white developers think. But this one is persistent."

Darrell nodded. "I got that from him. And there was something else." He looked down at Tess.

"Um," she said, and cleared her throat. "When Darrell got back from the beach this morning, he smelled funny."

Gus stared hard at her. "Funny how?"

She sat up straighter and leveled a cool gaze at the old man. Darrell recognized that look; Tess had gone into network correspondent mode, falling back on her professional training to stave off a panic attack. His arm tightened automatically around her shoulders.

"Sometimes," she said, "when I meet a person with a personal connection to a god, I get a visual aura. I see their god or goddess around or behind or above them." She put one hand on Darrell's thigh and gave him a little smile. "The first time I met this guy, he had the head of a rabbit." Darrell grinned back at her as she went on. "But this is the first time I've ever experienced an olfactory aura. And I didn't even see the man. I was asleep when he approached Darrell on the beach."

"What did it smell like?" Gus asked again.

"Like he'd been rolling in something dead."

Gus's eyes widened. "Wendigo."

"I was afraid you'd say that," Darrell said. He kept his tone even, but his gut clenched.

Tess glanced back and forth between the two men. "What am I missing?" Then her eyebrows shot up. "Wait. Isn't a wendigo supposed to be some kind of zombie? We saw one in a horror movie a couple of weeks ago." She looked at Darrell. "You mean they're real?"

"As real as the gods," Gus said.

"But they're not like the one in the movie," said Darrell. "That one was fifteen feet tall, thin as a rail, and with a bottomless hunger for human flesh. That's a legend from before the white man came, when the Anishinaabe lived off the land and the water. Our people experienced periods of starvation, especially in late winter when food supplies ran low, and there was always the risk that someone would go crazy from hunger and cannibalize their dead. The old ones told us anyone who ate human flesh would turn into a wendigo. The stench was supposed to warn you that the monster was coming."

"But it's just a legend," Tess said. "A scary story. Yet you're saying wendigos are real?"

"Our monsters today are more subtle," Gus said. The corners of his mouth quirked up.

Darrell, too, smiled mirthlessly. "A guy named Basil Johnston, who's an Ojibwe scholar, has compared developers to wendigos. They have the same kind of insatiable hunger for whatever they can get their hands on, no matter the cost to humanity or to the environment."

"He didn't just compare them," Gus said. "He said they *are* wendigos. And he was right. Those men who bought Forest Beach from the YMCA back in the '80s and tore down the trees to make houses for millionaires? They were wendigos. They had that board of directors in their thrall. But the directors wouldn't listen to reason, and now all those trees are gone." The old man shook his head.

"It's funny that you mention Forest Beach," Darrell said. "Whitaker said he's looking for a summer home there. He talked about its wasted potential."

"I bet he's planning something bigger," Tess said. "I bet he wants to rip down the dunes or something."

"He can't rip down the dunes," said Darrell. "They're protected by state law."

"When has state law ever meant anything to a wendigo?" Gus asked. "You have to stop him, Darrell."

"Me?" Darrell protested. "But we're here on vacation. Why is it *my* job?"

"He came to you," said Gus.

Tess squeezed his thigh. "After all, you're a Potawatomi superhero."

She delivered the line with a smirk, but it was true, and all of them knew it. Darrell's heart sank. "He must have picked up on it somehow. I wondered why he bothered to get out of his car just to introduce himself." He grimaced. "I guess I need to talk to Nanabush."

"Good idea," said Gus. "He has fought wendigos before."

Darrell barked a laugh. "In His own inimitable way."

"You met a *what?*" Nanabush's rabbity ears stood straight up in alarm.

"A developer by the name of Graham Whitaker," said Darrell. "Gus thinks he's a wendigo."

Nanabush, culture hero of the Ojibwe, sat cross-legged on the floor of Tess and Darrell's living room. Behind Him, leaning against a wall with arms and legs crossed, was Morrigan, the Irish goddess of war. Tess hadn't called Her when Darrell called Nanabush, but She had taken it upon Herself to show up anyway. "What is this 'wendigo'?" She asked now.

"A miserable manitou," Nanabush said without turning around. "In the old days, wendigos were content with feasting on human flesh. Now they feast on human greed."

"You've fought them before, haven't You?" Darrell asked.

"Well, yeah. But that was back in the day, when all you had to do was bash them in the head with a club a few thousand times. These new guys...." Nanabush propped His elbows on His knees and rested His chin on His fists. "I don't think they'll be so easy to beat."

"There has to be a way," Tess said.

"Agreed," said Morrigan. "What is his objective?"

"I don't know," Darrell said. "He seemed to be interested in Forest Beach when I talked to him. But Gus said he's been nosing around the tribal property, too."

Nanabush sat up, a hard look in His eye. "We can't let him have it."

"Of course we can't."

"If we stop him at this Forest Beach," Morrigan suggested, "the rest will take care of itself."

Tess nodded and grabbed her tablet from the coffee table. "I'll check the county records. Maybe he's started buying up property or something."

"I'll call the tribal chairman," Darrell said. "He'll have more concrete information than Gus had." He stopped in the act of pulling out his phone. "What will You do, Nanabush?"

The god's head had drooped nearly to His chest. "Same thing I always do before I fight a wendigo," He said. "Panic."

Half an hour after the gods took their leave, Tess looked up at Darrell in triumph. "I was right. Lakefront Associates has been busy buying up property north of U.S. 12 from New Buffalo to the Indiana line."

"Houses?"

"Just vacant lots so far."

Darrell nodded. "He'll have a tough sell with the homeowners. Some of those summer homes have been in those families for generations. The Daleys still own a house in Grand Beach."

"Daley," Tess said. "Chicago's mayoral dynasty? *Those* Daleys?"

"Yes, those Daleys."

"Wow."

He leaned over to give her a kiss, and grabbed the car keys off the coffee table. "I couldn't get Alex on the phone, so I'm going to drive up to the tribal office. Want to come along?"

She glanced back at her tablet. "Can't. I need to call Tracie." Tracie was Tess's producer in the NWNN investigative unit. "The network has research resources that I can't get to on this thing. Or at least, not without paying hundreds of dollars for a subscription." She wrinkled her nose. "Why haven't the gods abolished capitalism, anyway?"

"Capitalism isn't evil," he said. "It's an economic system like any other economic system. All of them can be exploited by the unscrupulous."

She rolled her eyes at him. "The question was rhetorical, you know."

"I know." He kissed her again. "See you in an hour or so. We can head over to the casino for dinner."

"Okay," she said. "But I'm not picking up the check this time. So don't go thinking you can lose our dinner money on any one-armed bandits."

Tribal chairman Alex Peters glanced at Whitaker's business card and snorted with disgust as he handed it back to Darrell. "Yeah," he said. "I know the guy. What are you doing, getting mixed up with him? I thought your folks had raised you better."

Darrell raised his hands in surrender before taking back the card. "I'm not mixed up with him. I met him on the beach in New Buffalo this morning, that's all. Just seemed like there was something funny about him."

Alex snorted again. "I'll say."

"Gus thinks he's a wendigo," Darrell said, dropping his voice.

Alex gave him a measured look and said quietly, "He might be right. Come on in for a minute." He motioned toward his office. Once the door was shut and Darrell was seated, Alex said, "Tell me what you know."

Darrell recounted his meeting with Whitaker that morning, and added Tess's findings. "Gus told us this guy was trying to buy property from the tribe, too. Is that right?"

"Yep," Alex said. He sat back and crossed his arms. "That's right. About a year ago, he came nosing around here, wanting to buy the casinos."

Darrell's eyes widened. "All three of them?"

Alex nodded. "He had a particular interest in the one in New Buffalo, of course, since it's the biggest, and it's got the concert venue and the hotel attached. But he would have happily taken all three of them off our hands."

"I bet he didn't have any plans to put the casino profits back into the community the way we do, either."

"No bet," Alex said. "In fact, he said we were crazy to handle it like we have. We should be keeping all that money, he said. Building the business with it, he said. He could make that casino the biggest tourist destination in Michigan, Indiana, and Illinois. He'd even throw in Ohio as a bonus."

"And the council told him to take a hike."

"You bet we did."

"I assume he wasn't happy."

Another snort. "That's an understatement." Alex sat forward. "Darrell, I have never seen a guy so mad. I wouldn't have been surprised to see steam come out of his ears, like some cartoon character. That's how mad he was. And then he started talking *really* crazy — about how we'd be sorry we turned him down, and how he was gonna eat us for lunch."

Darrell blinked. "You mean 'eat our lunch.' Right?"

Alex slowly shook his head. "Nope. I said it right the first time. That was an exact quote."

Darrell went cold.

"Listen," Alex said in a confidential tone, leaning his forearms on his desk, "I heard some pretty crazy things about your activities in Washington a couple of years back."

Darrell felt his cheeks flush. "If you heard them from my cousin Mike, they're mostly true."

"He said you were some kind of superhero."

Darrell laughed self-consciously. "Yeah. He keeps calling me that."

"He also said you had a direct pipeline to the spirits."

"That much," Darrell said, "is true."

Alex nodded to himself. Then he said, "You've gotta help us get rid of this guy."

"That's why I'm here," Darrell told him. *Whether I want to be or not.*

Darrell gave Tess a full report as soon as he got back to the condo. But she made him wait until they got to the casino steakhouse that night before she told him about Tracie's results. "If it's the same guy," she said, "he's been trying to do deals all over the Great Lakes."

Darrell looked up from his menu. "Oh?"

"Yeah," she said. In a stage whisper, she continued, "And in Minnesota last year, he was charged with defrauding investors in connection with a big casino development. Took their money and skipped town. Never built the casino."

"That would explain where he got the funds to buy all those vacant lots," Darrell murmured. "Did he do time?"

"No," she said. "He was ordered to pay a fine and restitution. He paid the fine, all right, but the individual investors have filed suit to get their money back."

"Good luck to them," Darrell said as the waitress came by to take their order.

As she stepped away, Darrell saw Tess look past him. Her eyes went wide for a moment, and her mouth made a perfect O; then she plastered a professional smile on her face. He had half-turned in his chair to see who she was looking at when a heavy hand landed on his shoulder.

"Well, Mr. Warren, we meet again." Darrell looked up to see Graham Whitaker grinning down at him.

"Mr. Whitaker," he said, and stood, shrugging off the man's hand in the process. "Good to see you again. This is my fiancée, Tess Showalter."

"A pleasure," he said, reaching out to shake Tess's hand. She murmured something inaudible in response, and he turned back to Darrell. "This is twice in one day that we've run into one another. The fates clearly want us to meet."

"Clearly," Darrell replied. His guts were in the process of liquifying, but he stood his ground. "Here for dinner?"

"Best steaks in town," Whitaker said. Then, placing a hand next to his mouth, he said, "Which isn't saying much. Too many ticky-tacky chain restaurants around here. What this town needs is a world-class place or three."

"Really," Tess said. "And how would you suggest that the locals bring them in?"

"I'm working on that, Ms. Showalter," Whitaker said. He spread his arms wide and said grandly, "I have a vision for Harbor Country."

"Is it similar to the vision you had for Menominee, Wisconsin, Mr. Whitaker?" she asked. Her tone was mild, but Darrell felt the barb underneath. "And what about Duluth? Is it the same vision you had for your investors there?"

Whitaker's face darkened. He looked from Tess to Darrell and said curtly, "Enjoy your dinner." Then he turned on his heel and stalked to a nearby table, where several men were already seated.

Darrell resumed his seat. "Nothing like tipping our hand," he said.

"Fucker deserved it," she said shortly. She nodded at his table. "Probably wining and dining a whole new bunch of dupes as we speak."

Darrell couldn't disagree. He resisted the impulse to turn around and memorize the faces at Whitaker's table so he could warn them later. "How did you know it was him?"

Finally, her voice quavered. "The thing towered over him. And it was slavering blood." She picked up her water glass, held it for a moment, and put it down again without drinking from it. Her expression twisted. "I'm not sure I can eat dinner. Not in the same restaurant with him."

Darrell knew exactly how she felt; his own stomach had yet to settle down. He caught the waitress's eye and motioned her over. "Something's come up," he said, and asked her to bag up their meal.

"Of course," she said. Tess gave him a grateful look as she moved away.

A few minutes later, their meals in to-go boxes, they made their escape to the lobby. "Mr. Warren!" Whitaker called after them.

"Shit," Tess hissed as Darrell turned back to see Whitaker hurrying to catch them.

"Thank you for waiting," the man said as he reached them. "I wanted to apologize for my behavior. It was uncalled for."

"Not a problem," Darrell said.

"Oh, but it is to me. And I insist on making it up to you," Whitaker went on. "Do you fish? I'd love to take you both out on the lake for a day."

"I don't know," Darrell hedged, as Tess's eyes telegraphed her alarm. "Tess isn't very good on the water."

"Oh, I'm a very safe boater," Whitaker assured her. "Very safe. You'll hardly notice we're moving at all." He turned back to Darrell. "Good! Then we're all set. Meet me early tomorrow at the marina. Say, seven a.m.?"

"How will we find you?" Darrell asked, surrendering to the inevitable.

"My boat is called the Grand Bargain," he replied. "I'm at slip 32. See you then, Mr. Warren. Ms. Showalter." He nodded to them both and headed back into the restaurant.

"Shit," Tess said again. "I hope Nanabush has figured out a plan."

Darrell wrapped an arm around her shoulders as he watched the man's retreating back. "So do I," he said.

It was still pitch dark when Tess and Darrell pulled into the marina parking lot. Darrell killed the motor and they got out. The temperature had dropped below freezing overnight, and a cold wind, smelling of snow, blew in off the lake.

Tess shoved her hands deep into the pockets of her down jacket. "Jesus, it's cold," she said, her breath misting in front of her mouth. She glanced around. "Why do I feel like a target's painted on my back?"

"I sure hope Nanabush knows what he's doing," Darrell said.

The rabbit-eared god had showed up as they ate their takeout steaks the night before. He was ecstatic to hear of the fishing trip and encouraged them to go. "That's perfect," He had crowed. "On the lake is exactly where I want him to be."

Tess was dubious, but eventually agreed to play along. Now, here they stood, freezing in the pre-dawn darkness. "Let's get this over with," Darrell said. He took Tess's elbow, and together they headed for the slip where Whitaker's boat was docked.

The Grand Bargain was a forty-foot cabin cruiser with all the bells and whistles. The lights were on, and Whitaker stood at the stern.

"Permission to come aboard," Darrell called, out of habit.

"Granted, and welcome," Whitaker replied, as they stepped across onto the vessel and tried to look pleased to be there.

"Pretty late in the season for this," Darrell said.

"Are you kidding?" said Whitaker. "This is the best time of year for lake fishing. The fish are bulking up for the winter right now. They'll gobble the bait right off the hook." He rubbed his hands together, a predatory gleam in his eye. "I expect to catch some big ones today."

Darrell nodded. "I guess we'll see, won't we?"

Whitaker was already moving toward the helm. "There's breakfast in the galley," he called over his shoulder.

"Sounds great," Tess said, bolting for the stairs.

Below, they found a stainless steel coffeepot, a box of store-bought doughnuts, and a couple of mugs. Darrell felt the boat get underway as he took a sip of his coffee.

Tess made a face. "Tastes funny." Then she looked at him wide-eyed. "You don't think…."

"Nah. The water's just stale. It's probably been sitting in the holding tank since August." But he sipped again to be sure.

Eventually, they braved the deck again, joining Whitaker in the cockpit. "How far out are we going?" Darrell asked over the roar of the engine.

"We'll head up the coast a few miles," the man called back, "and then out to open water. I know a spot south of St. Joe where we should have some good luck." He flashed them a grin, even teeth gleaming faintly in the glow from the GPS.

Darrell looked at Tess huddled in her jacket, her knit hat pulled low on her forehead. "You okay?" he yelled in her ear.

"Okay," she yelled back. "Cold."

"Go back below," he told her. She nodded and headed for the ladder.

Darrell eased himself into the co-pilot's seat, the doughnut and coffee he'd consumed sitting uneasily in his stomach. The cockpit was glassed in on three sides with a curtain across the back, and there was a heater at his feet, but it was still a chilly way to spend a Saturday morning in late October. Whitaker, though, didn't seem to feel the cold. His head and hands were bare, and his leather jacket was open at the neck. He seemed to be singing something under his breath. Darrell listened carefully, and when he caught the words, his blood froze:

Oh! Oh! My burning feet of fire! Oh! Oh! My fiery height and speed!

Whitaker noticed Darrell staring at him and grinned fiercely.

Darrell snapped his mouth closed. With an effort to sound normal, he shouted over the engine noise, "Tell me about your plans for Forest Beach."

"Gonna build the biggest resort destination in the Midwest," Whitaker boomed. "It's a spectacular location, smack-dab between Detroit and Chicago. And the market is there. Money's already used to coming up here for the weekend – just need to give them something high-class to spend it on."

"Such as?" Darrell looked around as he spoke. No lights from shore were visible. He judged they were close to the middle of the lake, and he began to wonder where this fabulous fishing spot of Whitaker's was.

"Convention center," the man said. "Hotels, shopping – high street shops, not rinky-dink gift shops. Big casino on a cruise ship, docked in the lake right off the beach."

"The dredging for that won't come cheap," Darrell said. "And it's liable to wipe out quite a bit of the dunes. Can you get the environmental approval for it?"

"Only small minds worry about that kind of thing," Whitaker sneered.

The sun, blood-red, was coming up behind them. *Red sky at morning...* The rhyme came unbidden into Darrell's mind; with an effort, he blocked it out. "And the region already has several casinos. Are you sure your market's not tapped out?"

Whitaker glared at him. "Those damned Indians put you up to this, didn't they?"

"Sorry?"

"I know who you are," Whitaker said. "I checked you out. You're one of those Indians. But you're some kind of superhuman Indian, aren't you?"

"I don't know what you're talking about," Darrell said. The weather was turning, he noticed. The boat plowed through increasingly rough waters, and it was beginning to snow. Tiny flakes melted on the windshield and immediately refroze.

"And your girlfriend there," Whitaker went on, motioning toward the ladder. "I thought I recognized her. She's a whiz-bang reporter, huh?" He grinned evilly. "She'll make a tasty morsel."

Bear, Darrell's warrior totem, growled in his head. "Leave her alone," Darrell said, nearly adding, *if you know what's good for you.*

The snow had picked up rapidly; it sounded as if the boat were being pummeled by ice pellets.

"Those damned Indians will be sorry they didn't sell their casino to me," Whitaker said. "My operation will run them out of business. Then I'll be rich! Then they'll all be calling me – all those Indian tribes – begging me to run their casinos for them. But I'm going to set up my own operations instead. Keep all the money for myself." He let up on the gas suddenly and turned off the motor. The boat, buffeted by turbulent water, began to pitch and yaw. In the sudden quiet, Whitaker growled, "But first, I have to take care of you two."

"Don't do this," Darrell said. Suddenly, he was acutely aware that Whitaker had offered neither Tess nor him a life jacket.

Whitaker pulled a pistol from his jacket pocket. "Get up."

"We know what you are," Darrell said. "Nanabush is on His way."

Whitaker howled with laughter. "Nanabush! That sorry excuse for a god? He's too stupid and scared to be a threat to me!" He motioned with the gun. "I said, get up."

Darrell rose slowly and, hands raised, backed toward the stern. The full force of the storm hit him as soon as he was out from under the canopy: driving snow stung his face, and the boat's rocking made it hard to keep his feet.

"Get her up here," Whitaker said above the howling wind.

"Tess?" Darrell called. "Come on up."

"What?" she called. "Why did we stop?" Her head emerged from below. "Oh, shit," she said, as she took in the scene.

"That's right," said Whitaker. "Go ahead and join your boyfriend over there. Don't do anything stupid, or I'll have to use this."

"I wouldn't do it," Tess said as she walked unsteadily to Darrell across the pitching deck. "The gods are on to you."

"Shut up," Whitaker said. "Step over the side onto the swim platform. That's right."

A panicked Nanabush materialized behind Whitaker. Darrell glared at Him and said in his head, *Do something!* The god shrugged helplessly.

"Good," Whitaker said. "Now jump."

"We'll drown!" Tess cried.

"Now you're catching on," said Whitaker, training the gun on her.

"Nanabush!" Darrell yelled in frustration as he and Tess fought to keep their balance on the heaving platform.

Whitaker rolled his eyes. "Nice try," he sneered, and squeezed the trigger.

Out of nowhere, Morrigan appeared and lunged for Whitaker's arm. But Darrell couldn't tell whether She had been in time.

Tess shrieked and fell backward into the water. Darrell dove in after her.

He flashed back to the last time he'd had to dive into roiling water to rescue her. It had been summer then, and the hurricane-driven waters had been warmer. Now, the lake was breathtakingly cold, and Tess's down coat would not protect her. Hypothermia would set in almost immediately. He had to find her and get her to safety.

He barked a bitter laugh. There would be no safety. They were miles from shore. And unlike the last time, there was no flotilla of Navy boats standing by to rescue them. Their nearest refuge was the boat they'd just been forced from – a boat in the possession of a wendigo.

Still, he had to try.

He called on his other animal totem, Otter, and She responded immediately. His clothing felt warmer, more waterproof, and he stopped shivering. Unerringly, he dove for Tess, wrapped his flippers – no, his arms – around her, and dragged her to the surface. There, she gasped for breath as he fought to keep both their heads above the waves.

It was a losing battle. And Otter could extend no warmth or strength to Tess. Even if Darrell swam for shore, she would die of exposure before he could get her there.

Nanabush! he screamed in his head. *You have to get us out of here!*

All right, all right, the lop-eared god said, exasperated. *You don't have to yell.*

A moment later, Darrell and Tess sprawled on the floor of their rented condo.

Darrell blew out a breath. Then, his heart in his throat, he checked Tess for signs of blood loss. By the grace of one god or another, she appeared to have dodged Whitaker's bullet.

But that didn't mean she was out of danger. "Come on," he said. "We need to warm up, and fast. Let's get out of these wet clothes and into bed."

"Y-your pickup line needs w-work," she said through chattering teeth. He laughed weakly and pulled her to her feet.

Much later, they sat before the living room fireplace, sipping mugs of hot soup and watching the snow fall. "I wonder what happened to Whitaker," Tess said for about the tenth time.

Nanabush materialized, striking a casual pose at the breakfast bar. "Don't worry. I took care of him." The god breathed on the nails of one hand and buffed them on His buckskin tunic.

"Oh, please," Morrigan said, rolling Her eyes. Her leather armor creaked as She stalked toward Him, Her broadsword sheathed at Her back. "Tell them what really happened. Or I will."

"Killjoy," Nanabush muttered. "Fine. Our Celtic warrior goddess here subdued him and got the gun away from him. But he won't be coming back."

Darrell and Tess traded an amused look. "How'd you manage that?" Darrell asked.

"His boat foundered in the storm," Nanabush said with a straight face. "I expect it will run aground at South Haven in a day or two."

"And Whitaker?" Darrell asked. "Is his body aboard? Or will he be lost at sea?"

Nanabush and Morrigan traded a look.

By now, the twenty-second year since the gods' return to Earth, Darrell had seen Them express many emotions: joy, anger, compassion, humor, and disgust, to name a few. But he had never seen any of Them horrified.

Until now.

It was Morrigan who answered him at last. "There's no body," She said simply. "The wendigo ate him."

The Door into Summer

When the authors in the 559 Awesome Assembly of Authors Facebook group started kicking around ideas for Summer Dreams, *some of us latched onto the idea of using song titles as springboards for our stories. We used the same idea to better effect in another anthology later. But for this collection, which appeared in 2014, I riffed on the Monkees' song "The Door Into Summer" (and not, to be clear, the Heinlein story of the same name) and came up with this foray into magic realism.*

She looked out the window, scowling. This new day looked very much like the one before it. A cold rain beat against the casement, leaching color from everything as it fell, until it seemed her world had faded to shades of gray.

She sighed and contemplated calling out. She was certain her employer wouldn't notice her absence. She worked as an assistant to businessmen who didn't really need her assistance; they paid her very well for not doing very much. Her days largely consisted of looking busy.

It hadn't always been this way. She dimly recalled a time years ago, when the work had challenged her; she had looked forward, then, to getting up and going to her job, where she would answer the phone with a smile in her voice and would complete her tasks with alacrity and good cheer.

It seemed like a very long time ago.

She sighed again, and began to make her daily deals with herself. If she could find nothing suitable to wear, she would call out. If the sidewalks were icy, she would call out. If the bus came so early that she missed it, she would call out. If the train was too crowded, she would call out, and then turn around and head home.

But on this day, everything worked. All the little routines functioned efficiently, the way she had intended when she had set them up – back when she still cared. Her clothes fit; her boots clung to the sidewalk and kept her feet out of the wet; the bus was exactly on time; the train had empty seats. And so she found herself deposited far too soon on a gray downtown sidewalk near the office where she served out her self-induced indenture. Just a short walk in the cold rain now stood between her and her interminable workday.

She snapped open her umbrella and, head down, began to trudge toward her doom – a gray figure amongst a crowd of gray figures on this cold, gray morning.

Half a block later, she stopped, turned, and looked up. She had not been mistaken; from a doorway she had never noticed before, a soft, golden light shone upon the patch of sidewalk she had just crossed.

She glanced to either side; the stream of people parted around her as if she were a rock impeding their flow. It seemed that no one else had seen the golden light. Perhaps they couldn't. Perhaps they didn't care.

She realized that she cared very much. With slow, tentative steps, she approached the shining doorway.

To her surprise, the door stood open. Just past the threshold, a carpet of lush grass stretched away to the horizon. The golden light came from the sun, shining in a cloudless sky; it seemed almost to kiss her face, and warmed her hands as they clutched the handle of her umbrella. She heard birdsong and the chuckle of an unseen brook; now and again, she thought she caught a few bars of music from a pennywhistle band. Honeysuckle sweetened the air.

She had always loved the scent of honeysuckle.

She looked around again. There ought to be a crowd around this door, she thought. Was she the only one hungry for the kiss of sunlight and the scent of fresh air?

She glanced above the doorway. Cut into the wall above the lintel was a single word in curiously-shaped letters. It said, simply:

SUMMER

She blinked rainwater out of her eyes – at some point she must have lowered her umbrella – and looked through the doorway again. The scene had changed; now she beheld a line of brightly painted wagons – gypsies, she fancied – in a wildflower meadow. The smell of roasting meat made her mouth water. An unseen fiddler played sweetly, his tune pulling at her feet to join the dance.

It was the tug at her feet that recalled her to herself. She snatched up her umbrella as if she had been propositioned – for in a sense, she had – and stalked purposefully away from the door.

The rest of the way to her office, her steps lagged only once. As she turned the corner, she glanced back up the street almost furtively. Sure enough, the golden glow was still there, spilling out onto the sidewalk. And still, no one else seemed to notice.

She shook her head and walked away.

That whole day at her desk, she puzzled over the doorway full of light. Was it real, or had she been hallucinating? Perhaps her subconscious mind had conjured up the experience as an antidote to her pointless life.

Perhaps it was real, but an advertisement for some new product. A laundry detergent, perhaps, in a sunshine-and-honeysuckle scent. Or a show at one of the local theaters. Or an exhibit at the zoo.

Of course. That must have been it. It was simply an ad of some sort. That would explain why no one else seemed to notice it; they had all seen it before.

Satisfied, she turned back to her work. But still, she felt a nagging sense of loss. Why had she not simply stepped through the door? Entering the shop – if shop it was – would have answered all her questions. But she hadn't even tried.

Well, she reasoned, she had been on her way to work. If she had entered the shop, she would very likely have been late. Just because she found her work pointless and boring didn't mean she didn't need the money. She could not afford to lose her job.

That's all very fine, a voice inside her head said. *But you could step out at lunchtime and have a look. There's no danger of losing your job if you go out for a bite, as long as you're back within the hour.*

She knew that voice: it was the voice of temptation. In her younger days, she had heeded it often – sometimes to her sorrow. Since then, she had schooled herself to ignore it. But on this particular morning, she was finding it difficult to ignore.

She cast an eye toward the staff lounge, where the sensible lunch she had packed the night before was stowed in the refrigerator. She almost never went out for lunch; she certainly had no tangible reason to do so today.

And yet.

The possibility tantalized her all morning. But in the end, she fetched her packed lunch from the refrigerator and ate it at her desk at the usual time.

That afternoon, the voice started in on her again. *You must pass the shop on your way to the train station,* it reminded her. *What harm would there be in stopping in on your way home?*

What harm, indeed? But perhaps the shop would be closed then.

She made a deal with herself: if the shop were open that evening when she left work, she would go inside.

But on her way home, she could not find the door. She was certain of the location; it could only have been in one particular spot in one specific city block. But it wasn't there. It was as if the shop had never existed at all.

Now she was sure she had hallucinated the whole thing. Frowning at herself, she went on to the train station and headed for home.

A few days later, it happened again.

Another cold, gray morning – this time with a leaden fog enveloping the world. She awoke feeling as if she were wrapped in cotton batting gone dingy with age. Even before she got out of bed, she began to make deals with herself: If the room is too cold when I throw back the covers, I'll call out. If I haven't enough milk for my cereal, I'll call out. If I can't find my umbrella, I'll call out.

Of course, the heat was working, she had sufficient milk, and the umbrella was right where she had left it. When the bus loomed out of the fog, she was at the bus stop, waiting for it.

Even the sound of the subway seemed muffled as it pulled into the station. She dragged herself onto the jammed train and stood, her face mashed miserably into someone's armpit, all the way to work.

The fog was even thicker in the city. The air seemed viscid, as if she were slogging through gelatin. Putting one foot in front of the other on the sidewalk seemed to take a monumental effort. She wondered whether the going would be any easier if she turned around and went back to the subway; she fancied that perhaps the path she had already forged through the thick air had not yet closed behind her. But onward she plodded, step by sluggish step.

Then she stepped into a circle of golden light.

With a gasp of surprise, she looked to her right. There was the doorway with the curious sign above it. Again, the door was open, and the sunlight streaming through it from beyond seemed almost to beat back the fog.

She looked around at her fellow commuters. As before, none appeared to notice the luminous doorway.

Timidly, she approached. This time, she beheld an English-style garden. Flowers nodded in their beds, animated by a soft breeze: lilies and petunias, marigolds and anemones and snapdragons. A fountain splashed in the center of the scene, its cherubic fixtures seeming to beckon to her. Beyond, rose blooms covered a trellis, shading an inviting stone bench. The sunlit air smelled of boxwood and clover.

She had always loved snapdragons.

Without conscious thought, she took a tentative step toward the scene; the toe of her boot touched the grass and sank into the luxurious turf. Clear water trickled from the edge of the grass, dampening the pavement around her shoe.

It was the trickle of water that made her draw back. She could not afford to be so entranced. She could not! She had to get to work. She could not afford to lose her job.

With a heavy sigh, she laid one hand on the door frame and withdrew her foot from the threshold. Resolutely, she turned away.

But as she made her way through the dank fog, she dashed away tears of frustration and loss. How had she gotten herself into such a state – one in which she must forego opportunity because of duty? She had always been the responsible sort. She prided herself on her steadiness, her dependability. She did what she was supposed to do and rarely bent the rules. Why did life never allow her to have fun?

It wasn't Life, she realized as she sat at her desk at last. It was her. She herself curtailed any opportunities for fun. She never took vacations, preferring to stay home with a book on her days off. The characters in the novels she read had adventures in her stead; they took all the risks, while she stayed safely on her sofa with a mug of tea. Love and hate, joy and despair, anger and desolation – she felt them all at a remove, and when she was in danger of feeling them too much, she simply closed the book.

She led a safe life. But it was never spontaneous, and it was very rarely fun.

She determined that if the golden door was still there when she left work that evening, she would step through it.

But when she walked back to the train station, the door had disappeared. It was as if it had never been there at all. She did not realize she was sobbing, standing in the middle of the sidewalk where the door should have been, until someone touched her elbow and asked whether she was all right.

"No," she blubbered – so uncharacteristic of her! As she fished in her purse for a tissue, she decided to take a chance with this stranger. "No, I am not all right. Tell me: have you ever seen a store called Summer in this block?"

The man let go of her elbow and took a step back. "No, ma'am," he said. "I've never heard of that store."

"It was here this morning," she said, almost pleading, as she dabbed at her nose. "The door was open, and the most wonderful golden light came through it and dispelled all the fog near the door. Are you sure you've never seen it?"

"No, ma'am," he said again, and now she caught the wary look in his eye.

Of course. He thinks I'm crazy. "Never mind," she said, and made an effort to smile. "I must have the wrong block. Thank you for your kindness." Without another word, she pivoted and walked rapidly away, toward the train station.

It was not until she got home, safe behind her door, that she allowed herself the luxury of tears again.

In the days that followed, the air turned bitterly cold. She wrapped herself each morning in layer upon layer of wool and down before heading out to the bus stop, but the warmth never reached her heart. She found herself longing for another glimpse of the golden light. Alas, the elusive storefront did not appear.

Now and again, she would see the man to whom she had blurted her confusion. He was not one of the regular homeless people, who sat at the same spot every day and asked incessantly for spare change; she always averted her eyes from them. This man never panhandled – or at least, she never saw him do it. There was a noble air about him, she thought; he always stood a little apart from the others in his threadbare tweed jacket, hands stuffed in the pockets of his worn jeans as he nodded gravely at the commuters. He could almost be a university professor, or a scientist – someone who did not care about appearances. But a professor or a scientist would not spend most mornings on a city street corner, greeting those who acknowledged his presence by sparing him a glance.

Once or twice, he had nodded to her. The first time, she had looked away immediately, as if caught out in a social faux pas. The next time, though, she nodded carefully back, returning his acknowledgement with a distant nod of her own.

Then it snowed. Fat flakes drifted out of the sky as she made her breakfast; she watched them pile up on the grass as she ate. She began to make her deals with herself: if her boots weren't warm enough, she would call out. If the snow was up to her ankles, she would call out. If the storm appeared to be settling in, so that her commute home would be a nightmare, she would call out for the day.

But the forecast called for snow only through midday, her feet stayed warm, and the sidewalks were just damp. The wet concrete reminded her, as she walked to the bus stop, of the rivulet of water that had sprung from the grass in the doorway of the mysterious shop.

As she came up from the subway at her accustomed stop, she glanced toward where the noble homeless man often stood – a glance, she realized, that had become a habit with her. But he wasn't there. Instead, he stood at the top of the escalator. He seemed to be searching the faces of the commuters with some urgency. Then he saw her.

"Ma'am," he said, as she came level with him. "May I speak with you for a moment?"

She glanced around, but there appeared to be no way out. Nodding stiffly, she followed him around to the side of the station, out of the way of people hurrying to work.

The storm had intensified in the few minutes she had been on the train; the flakes were smaller now, and driven by a sharp wind. It was difficult to see across the street. The two of them seemed to her to share a cocoon of cotton batting.

He turned to her then and said simply, "I saw it."

His words did not register at first; her attention was caught by the snowflakes melting on his dishwater-blond curls. "Where's your hat?" she said, more sharply than she had intended.

"I can't wear a hat."

"Why not?"

He raised one hand above his head. "My head needs to breathe so I can hear the messages."

She was nonplussed. *He's crazy*, she thought, as she looked for a polite escape route.

"Did you hear me?" he said, touching her elbow, making her flinch. He ignored her reaction, or didn't notice; in any case, he plowed on. "I saw it. This morning. I saw your store."

All her ruminations on the possible impairment of his mental state had fled. "You saw the golden doorway?"

He nodded emphatically. "When it first started snowing. I was wrapped up in my quilt, trying to sleep in a doorway across the street. It was so cold that I all I could do was doze, off and on. But then something woke me up. *Really* woke me up. I think it might have been the light." He nodded again, to himself this time. "It might have been the light, at that." He focused on her again. "So I crossed the street and took a good look inside the door. It looked just the way you said it would: a warm, sunny meadow with sheep grazing in the distance."

Her nascent smile froze. Sheep? She had never told him what she saw. And in any case, she had never seen sheep through the doorway. But then, she had never seen the same scene twice, either.

"Anyway," he said, as her silence lengthened, "I wanted you to know that somebody else had seen it. In case you thought you were crazy before." He shoved his hands in his jeans pockets and turned to go.

"Wait!" she said, snapping out of her stasis. She reached out to him; the fabric of his jacket felt nubbly under her fingers. "Is it still there?"

He glanced at her hand on his arm and smiled. "Let's go see." Together, they crossed the street, the snow whorling and eddying around them.

It was gone. She knew it even as they began walking down the block. The doorway should have shone as a beacon through the blizzard, but it simply was not there.

They stopped as one, peering in silent dismay at the place where the doorway should have been.

In a moment, though, her disappointment faded as a thought occurred to her. "Why didn't you go in last night?" she asked. "You could have. You have no ties here – no job, no house, nothing to hold you back. Or at least, I assume that's the case." When he nodded faintly, she went on, "And it was so cold. *You* were cold. And it was warm inside. Why didn't you go in?"

He looked at her as if the answer were self-evident. "I couldn't go without you," he said.

She didn't know what to say. Finding her voice at last, she said, "You don't even know me."

"I know you're sad," he said. "You always look sad. I wanted to see you smile."

She knew she was staring at him. "I have to go to work," she mumbled finally, and pulled away.

The day never regained its equilibrium. Several times, she found herself near to tears. At one point, she felt as if she was going to hyperventilate; she ran to the bathroom and hid in the farthest stall, bent nearly double while she breathed into her cupped hands.

"Are you okay?" her boss when she returned to her cubicle. "You're as white as a sheet."

"Fine," she said, waving away his concern and resuming her seat. "I'm fine. Really." But he didn't appear to believe it any more than she did.

That afternoon, she attended a retirement party for a co-worker. There were the usual speeches about a job well done, a rest well earned. But her co-worker seemed almost frightened. "It's a big step," the woman said, "leaving here. For decades, my life has been structured around this place. I'm losing an anchor."

"But gaining your freedom," another co-worker said.

The near-retiree laughed nervously. "I don't even know what that means."

She smiled and moved away to the refreshments. As she approached the buffet, she spotted some former co-workers – retirees now – who had returned for the party. She observed them curiously. There was something odd about them, she thought. They seemed…happy. Yes, that was it: they were relaxed and happy.

She excused herself and went back to her cubicle. There, she wrote a note, folded it, placed it in an envelope, and left it on her boss's desk. She donned her coat and hat. Then she reached up slowly, removed her hat, and placed it in a drawer. She no longer needed it; it was too late to keep the messages out.

While she had spent her day indoors, the storm had moved on, and the sky had turned a brilliant blue. Traces of snow still clung in the shadows, but the day had warmed and most of the morning's snowfall had melted away. It was, she realized, a beautiful day. And yet she was not surprised when she rounded the corner and saw golden light spilling across the sidewalk halfway up the block. Nor was she surprised to see her homeless man standing next to the doorway.

He smiled when he saw her, and held out his hand to her. "I waited for you," he said. "My name's Lucas, by the way."

"I'm Hannah," she said, and put her hand in his. Together, they stepped through the door.

Daydream Believer

When we used the song-title-as-inspiration idea for I Heard It on the Radio *in early 2016, I turned once again to the Monkees — as well as to the mentoring program the administrators at my day job had recently begun to implement.*

"Whose idea was this?" I muttered, watching the bright-eyed sprite as she ordered her soy caramel macchiato or whatever it was. I have never been able to figure out what any of that junk on the menu sign means.

She finished ordering and I paid the man, and we moved to the pickup window to wait for her drink. I already had mine. I always order regular old American coffee. Nobody has to do anything goofy to it. You tell the cashier you want coffee, and he pours some in a cup and hands it to you. Simple.

I'm a simple guy, really. Which might have been why I was grumbling about having to be here with kid who was young enough to be my daughter.

I wouldn't have been here at all except it came up in my annual review last week. "Ray, you've worked here for thirty-five years," Moe, my supervisor, said. "That's your whole working life, unless I miss my guess."

"Except for delivering newspapers when I was a kid, yeah," I said.

"And you're reliable. And your output is damn near perfect."

"That's what the company pays me for."

"Right. But there's a company culture, too, and you don't ever participate in it." He raised a hand, forestalling my objections. "Now, I understand why you wouldn't want to go to some of these social get-togethers. It's not like you have a lot in common with the kids we're hiring these days."

"You got that right," I said. *Not to mention that I spend too many hours a day with the people I work with already.* But I didn't tell him that. I haven't lasted thirty-five years in this job by being stupid.

"But you have a lot of institutional wisdom in that noggin of yours," Moe went on, tapping the side of his head.

"Yeah? So?"

"So," he said, "the big boss wants us to start a mentor program. He wants us to pair off some people who have been here a long time with some of the newbies. Just, you know, take 'em out for coffee or something."

"Coffee?" I spluttered.

"Or something," he said. "Give 'em a call every now and then. See how they're doing. See if they have any questions you can answer."

I squinted at him. "Why?"

"Well," and here he sat back in his chair and looked uncomfortable, "we're having a little problem with retention."

"Pay 'em more money," I said. "That usually makes 'em want to stick around."

"You're a funny guy," he said, with a warning look in his eye. "Anyway, so we're going to try this mentor thing, and I've already picked out your mentee." He handed me a slip of paper. "Here's her contact info. Call her when you get back to your desk."

I recognized the name on the paper right away. She'd just been assigned to a project team I was on. I gave him the hairy eyeball and said, "This is a joke, right?"

"What do you mean?"

I couldn't believe he didn't get it. "I can't take this little slip of a thing out for coffee, Moe! Millie would kill me." Millie's the wife, by the way. We'll be married thirty years next month.

"It's not a date. It's a work assignment. Look." He leaned forward and rested his hairy forearms on his desk. "The big boss thinks if we pair off these kids with long-time employees, they'll feel more welcome. Then maybe they won't think of this place as a pit stop on the way to bigger and better things." He shrugged. "Maybe they'll start to envision themselves being here for a long time themselves."

I snorted. "Dream on, buddy." I looked at the paper he'd handed me again. "All right, I'll do it. But if Millie throws a fit, I'm sending her to you."

"Feel free," he said. He seemed relieved that I'd gone for it. But what else was I supposed to do? Say no and get fired?

So here we were, me and Ariel Plotnick, sitting at one of those stupid little round things they call tables in these places. When I said Ariel was tiny, I meant it. She didn't even come up to my shoulder. Might have weighed a hundred pounds soaking wet. She had a pointy nose and chin, and she looked at me out of green eyes, from under red-brown hair that was cut in what my mother used to call a pageboy. And there I was, a balding white guy in khakis and a sport shirt that had started the day neatly pressed.

"So, uh, Ariel," I said. "How's the job going so far?"

"Fine." She beamed at me. "Everyone is really nice. And the project we're working on is so interesting!"

"Yeah," I said.

She cocked her head. "You don't think so?"

"Well," I said, "I've done a few of these in my time, and..." Then I shut up. I had to remind myself not to say what I was really thinking – that every time in the past I'd been handed an assignment like this, it had been such a cock-up that I was lucky to get out of it in one piece. "And it will be interesting to see how this one turns out," I said instead.

"I think it's going to be amazing," she said.

She said it with conviction – like there was no other choice. "Oh?" I said. "What makes you say that?"

"Because it will be." She spread her hands in the air as if drawing a marquee. "I can see it now. We're going to pull it out at the last minute, and Moe will be so thrilled with our work that he'll give us all a promotion." She grinned, then sipped her drink.

"Really?" I said. This kid had a head on her shoulders, although I couldn't see myself buying into her optimism. "Will he give us all a raise, too?"

"Sure!"

I chuckled at her and shook my head. "That's a nice fantasy you've got going there."

She set down her drink and leaned in. "Can I let you in on a secret?"

"Depends on the secret."

"I believe in daydreams. If I can envision it, I can make it happen." She tapped the side of her head – the same thing Moe had done the day before.

Which reminded me of my *institutional wisdom*, as he'd called it. "That old 'think positive' thing, huh?" I shook my head. "I don't know that we'll be able to positive-think our way out of this one."

"I guess we'll see, won't we?" she said.

Over the next few weeks, the project turned into a cock-up, just as both Ariel and I had expected it would. One by one, the people on the team got more and more dejected. We'd all seen it happen before, and here it was, happening again.

Except for one thing. Usually, when things started going south, somebody would make a smart remark about it. You know, your garden-variety sarcasm – "oh, that's a beautiful thing," when it wasn't beautiful at all. And then someone else would try to top him, and before you knew it, we were all saying rotten things about the mess we had on our hands.

But Ariel took every one of our sarcastic remarks at face value. "It *is* beautiful!" she'd say, and then go on about how we could make it even more beautiful, if only we did this or that to it. It sounded like a fairy tale – except she was serious. The things she suggested would actually make the project better. And when someone – okay, it was usually me – would explain to her why we couldn't afford to do it that way, she'd suggest a way to do it differently.

And then someone else on the team would come up with an even better idea. Cheaper. More efficient. Something.

Damn her, she was making us into a success.

I didn't know how I felt about that. I'd spent thirty-five years at the company with the mindset that it was a job. Get up, do the work, go home. My job wasn't my life. My life was Millie and our dogs. We have four – did I mention that? They're all mutts from the pound, but Millie loves them. She calls them our babies, and I guess they kind of are, in a way.

We never had kids of our own. Millie couldn't.

Anyway, the point is that I never wanted to be best pals with any of my co-workers. I was there to do the job they hired me to do, period. I never wanted to be a star. Stars burn out.

A couple of weeks later, I couldn't take it any more. So I took Ariel out for coffee again – as her mentor, you understand. And once we were seated – me with my American joe and her with her fizzy fruity tea thing – I told her to ratchet it back.

She stopped pulling on her straw in mid-slurp and stared at me, big-eyed. "Why?"

"Because you're setting these guys up for a big disappointment," I said. "Look, I've been around the block a few more times than you have. You've got everybody hyped up about how we're going to be a big success, but projects like this always fall through at the last minute. There's always a fatal flaw in the plan."

"Where?" she said. "This time, I mean. We've all been over these plans every day for the past two months, and every time we bump up against a new problem, we solve it."

I shook my head. "I don't *know* where the big flaw is," I said. "If I knew, we could fix it right now. But I just know it's gonna happen."

"Because it always has."

"Yes. That's exactly right." I don't know why I felt like I had to convince her that we would fail, but I did.

She crossed her legs and leaned forward, balancing one elfin elbow on her knee. "Ray, what's your big dream?"

"That's an awfully personal question, Ariel," I said. "And I have a strict policy about keeping my personal life…"

She broke in. "Separate from work. I've noticed. It's kind of hard not to." She made a face, with her eyebrows way up and with one side of her mouth pulled up in sort of a half-smile. "So let's keep it focused on work. What's your ultimate goal, here? What's your dream?"

"Well…" I'd never given the question much thought before. "Retirement, I guess."

"And how many more years before you can retire?"

"Ten."

"And what happens then?"

I shrugged. "I won't have to work any more."

"No, I mean…" She looked off into space for a moment – searching for another way to put her question, I guess. Then she looked at me again. "When you're retired, what will make you get out of bed?"

"Millie," I said instantly, and laughed. "She won't tolerate it if I try to sleep all day. She'll make sure I get up in the morning."

"To do what?"

I blinked. "I…don't know."

"Well, think about it," said Ariel. "When you've figured it out, let me know." She sucked up the last of her drink noisily. "We should head back to work, huh?"

I followed her out the door, thinking about what she'd said. It wasn't until a couple of hours later that it dawned me that I'd gone to the coffee shop with an agenda, and she'd derailed me. She had no intention of ratcheting anything back.

I wanted to be mad at her, but I couldn't stop thinking about the challenge she'd posed me. What *did* I intend to do after I retired?

I knew what Millie wanted to do. She wanted us to move to the country, where we could have a little house with a lot of land for the dogs. Now and then, she would look at property online, and she'd always show me the places she liked the best. I always told her we didn't have the money.

But we did. If we sold our current place, we'd have plenty of money for any of the places Millie liked. So why was I digging my heels in? God knew it wasn't because I loved my job or my co-workers, or even our current neighborhood. It wasn't like family held us here – our parents were all dead, and her sister lived on the other coast. Was it because I didn't want to think about how much our lives would change? Or was it because Millie's dream wasn't mine?

A couple of weeks later, we wrapped up the project – and for the first time I could remember, it wasn't a cock-up. Not even close. It was actually beautiful. It was, as Ariel had said to me the first time we went out for coffee, *amazing*.

And as Ariel had predicted, Moe loved it. He didn't give us all promotions, but we each got a letter of commendation from the big boss. And a bonus. A pretty hefty one.

This time, she invited *me* out for coffee. She picked the place – a diner where they serve pancakes, eggs any style, and real American joe. You tell the guy you want coffee and he pours you a cup. Simple.

"So what are you going to do with your big payout?" I asked her after we'd ordered. "Gonna take it and run to a better company?"

"Nah," she said, stirring sugar into her cup. "I like it here. The people are all really nice and the work is interesting. And hey, I'm a rising star now, right?"

"Be careful with that star talk," I advised her. "Stars burn out."

"But not for years and years," she said, and sipped her coffee.

"Good?" I asked.

"Needs whipped cream." She grinned archly. "So, Ray, what are you gonna do with your bonus? Have you figured out what your big dream is?"

"You know, it's funny," I said, "but I've been giving it a lot of thought since you asked me that."

"And?"

I wrapped my hands around the plain white mug. "Millie – that's the wife, you know."

"I know," she said. "Go on."

"Well, Millie's always wanted a big place in the country for the dogs," I said. "And for years, I've been putting her off, and I never thought about why it was."

"Don't leave me in suspense," she said, leaning in. "Why was it?"

"Well, I had to think about it. And I realized it was because I don't want just the dogs. I want horses. And chickens and cattle and all that stuff."

She smiled in delight. "You want to be a farmer? Really? That's so cool!"

"Is it?" I shook my head. "I don't know. I grew up on a farm. I guess it gets into your bones." I took a sip from my cup. "So anyway, I finally broke down and told Millie, and it turns out that she'd always known that's what I wanted. So I said to her, I said, 'Why didn't you tell me?'"

Ariel's green eyes shone. "What did she say?"

"She said she figured once we got out there, she could ease me into it." I shook my head again, and downed about half of what was in my cup.

"That's so cool," Ariel repeated. "So now what?"

"Well, now we're looking for a place. And if we find one before I'm eligible for retirement, I might just quit early. We can live on the proceeds from our house while we get the farm up and running." I glanced at her. "I mean, a lot of this is theoretical right now. We'll need to be careful that we don't lose our shirts."

"But now you've got the dream," she said. "Believe in it. That's all you need to make it happen."

And damn it if she wasn't right. I mean, it's been a lot of hard work, getting the farm running. But once I made the decision, everything fell into place. We found the perfect piece of property, put an offer on it, signed the papers, and found a buyer for our house in the suburbs – all in the same week.

When I told Ariel I was retiring, she hugged me. It felt good. Like I'd made a friend.

We still keep in touch – she's in middle management now, and dreaming about having one of those corner-office jobs. Maybe I should warn the big boss, huh?

Back Home Again

Airports, I think, are liminal spaces – *bridges between our day-to-day lives and whatever awaits us at the other end of the flight. The setting for this story is true, more or less; I was waiting for a flight at Reagan National Airport when I heard someone playing the Indiana University alma mater and "Back Home Again in Indiana" on a French horn. When I tracked the guy down, he really was wearing a straw boater and spats. From there, however, the story divulges. This piece appeared in the April 2015 issue of* 559 Monthly.

Flying never agrees with me. First, there's the peculiar scent common to commercial airplanes: that mix of canned air, off-gassing, and old barf that always makes me a teeny bit nauseous. I'd gotten a whiff of it as I walked past an open jetway door on the way to my gate, and my stomach was already clenching as I sat down to wait for my flight.

I downed a couple of anti-nausea pills with Diet Coke and dove deep into Facebook, in an effort to distract myself not only from the journey at hand, but also from what would be facing me at my destination: cleaning out my mother's condo. Her mind was starting to go, and she knew it. So my older sister, Janie, and I had talked her into assisted living – and to pay for it, we would have to sell the condo. Mom was okay with that. "It's not like I have any sentimental attachment to this place," she had told me in one of her lucid moments.

"Yeah, I know," I said. She and Dad had downsized to the condo from the house Janie and I grew up in. That had been two decades ago, and Dad had died shortly thereafter.

"I just wish your father was here to help."

"Yeah, I know, Mom. So do I."

"When's he getting home, anyway?"

I sighed. Her windows of lucidity were getting shorter. Janie lived closer to her than I did, and so she had shouldered most of the burden of caring for Mom. But she couldn't keep doing it – she had health issues of her own. And I lived too far away.

As I checked out statuses on my phone, I became dimly aware of an unusual sound amid the airport's din: a French horn, playing first one old-timey song, then another. A school band on an outing? Then why hadn't they checked their instruments? I was pretty sure a French horn case wouldn't fit into an overhead bin.

I shrugged and went back to my phone. But my head snapped up when I recognized one of the songs: my college *alma mater.*

What in the world…? I stashed the phone and followed the sound to its source: not a high schooler at all, but an old fellow with a long face, wearing a straw boater and spats, and tapping his toe as he played.

When he stopped to take a breath, I approached him. "Excuse me," I said, "but were you just playing the Indiana University school song?"

His face split in a grin. "There you are!" he cried happily. "Right this way!" And he got up, still playing – the tune this time was *Back Home Again in Indiana* – and led me through the crowd to a doorway with no number above it.

"Wait!" I cried. "I'm supposed to be flying to Chicago."

He turned and winked. "This is a shortcut." Then he took the horn in one hand and pushed the door open with the other. "Go on. They're waiting for you."

"But…." I turned back toward where my flight was supposed to be boarding, but I couldn't see the gate because of the throng. I turned back to the man with the horn. He smiled amiably and jerked his head toward the open doorway. I peered down the jetway and inadvertently took a whiff.

No airplane smell.

A shortcut with no canned air? I didn't wait for him to tell me again. I dashed down the hall and rounded the corner, where a set of steps led down to the tarmac.

I almost went back up the jetway. I got along with small planes even less well than I did with big ones. But I gritted my teeth and headed down the steps.

The steps led to concrete, all right. But not at the airport. Instead, I found myself on the sidewalk in front of my childhood home. Laundry was hanging on the line to dry, and our old Dodge Dart was parked in the driveway in front of the open garage door.

Then my father – who had been dead for nearly twenty years – stepped out of the garage.

I couldn't move. I couldn't even open my mouth to call his name.

He frowned and came toward me. "Something I can help you with, miss?" he asked.

I finally got my mouth open, but nothing would come out of it.

"You must be the house appraiser," he said. "Odd that they'd send a girl, but…. Anyway, come on in." He turned and walked away from me, toward the front door. As he held the door open and beckoned me inside, I flashed on a memory of the French horn player standing in much the same pose just a few moments before. I didn't know what was going on, but I was in this far. And anyway, I wanted to see the old house again.

"May!" Dad called as he followed me in. "The appraiser's here."

Mom came out of the kitchen, drying her hands on a towel. I'd last seen that towel in the rag bag, but here it was nearly brand-new. "Hello, dear," Mom said, extending her hand to me. "What's your name?"

"Sarah," I blurted.

"Oh, what a nice name! One of our daughters is named Sarah. Isn't that right, Sam?" Mom turned her thousand-watt smile on me, and I basked in it. It had been a long time since I had seen her so happy. Pretty much ever since Dad's death, in fact. "Now, what do you need for us to do?"

"Nothing," I said quickly. "I'll just take a look around and…appraise. The house." I nodded my head solemnly, as if I knew what I was doing. The truth was that I had no idea what an appraiser did. I'd never owned a piece of real estate in my life. But I had some vague inkling that I was supposed to be figuring out how much the house was worth, so that my parents knew how much to charge for the place when they sold it.

Neither Janie nor I had been on board with the idea of our parents selling the house. It wasn't just the sentimental value, although that played a part, too. But we were sure our folks wouldn't be happy in a condo. Dad loved tinkering in the garage, and Mom loved gardening and canning the produce she grew out back. Those activities were central to who they were.

When we voiced our concerns to our parents, Mom scoffed at us. "They're just hobbies," she said. "We'll find new hobbies. Won't we, dear?"

I could still remember the look of uncertainty in Dad's eyes when he replied, "Of course, we will."

Of course, they never did. Mom took over a community garden plot, but it was a lot harder to get to than our backyard plot had been, and there was nowhere to store her tools at the site. And she wasn't as young as she used to be. And their new kitchen didn't have enough counter space for her canning operation. She tried it for just one year, got frustrated, and gave up.

As hard as it was for Mom to walk away from gardening, Dad paid the higher price. He had always been a tinkerer, and even held a couple of patents. When he lost his workshop, he seemed to shrivel, and then to give up on life. He died in his sleep several months later. The doctor called it a coronary, but Janie and I agreed that his real cause of death was a broken heart.

I knew then what I needed to do.

I made a show of looking in all the closets. I pretended I didn't know how to get up in to the attic, and allowed Dad to pull down the stairs for me. I looked in all the bedrooms, complimented Mom on a crewel wall hanging that I myself had made in high school, asked about the plumbing and heating. Dad volunteered that the roof was nearly new, which was more or less the truth. Then I walked around the outside of the house, nodding thoughtfully, and poked my head into the garage. I confess that I asked Dad about the project he was working on just to see his eyes light up with pleasure.

I strung it out as long as I could. Then I went back into the house so I could talk to them both at once. Mom and I sat opposite each other at the kitchen table, and Dad propped one shoulder against the wall nearby.

"Mr. and Mrs. Ives," I began, but Dad interrupted me.

"You didn't take any notes," he said, his tone accusatory. "Are you sure you'll be able to give us a decent appraisal?"

"Not to worry," I said blithely. "I have a well-trained memory. I'll send you my report in due course. But may I offer you a completely unprofessional opinion first?"

Mom's eyes narrowed at that, but Dad said, "Sure. Go ahead."

"I don't think you should sell."

"That's none of your business," Mom said tartly.

"You're absolutely right," I said. "But I'll be honest with you, Mr. and Mrs. Ives. I've done a number of appraisals over the years for couples who were about your age." I sounded so authoritative that I half-believed myself. "I assume you're planning to downsize, am I correct? Maybe move into a condo?" At Mom's nod, I went on, "I thought so. But I can always tell when a couple like yourselves are attached to a place. That garden out back? That's a labor of love, unless I miss my guess."

"I'll get a community plot," Mom said. "I'm already on the waiting list."

"I've heard that before. But it won't be the same." I shook my head. "A community plot isn't nearly as convenient as walking out into your own backyard. I give you a year before you give it up." Then I turned to Dad. "And your workshop? You won't have space for it in a condo."

"We saw one building where there was a shop in the basement," he said.

"I bet you have to reserve it," I said. "You can't just go down there any old time you please."

I could tell he was wavering. But Mom snapped, "Did our daughters put you up to this? They've been after us not to sell."

"No, ma'am," I said, crossing my fingers under the table. "I don't even know your daughters."

Mom still looked suspicious. Dad glanced between us, and pushed himself away from the wall. "Well, thanks for your advice. We'll think it over."

I realized I'd done all I could do. I stood and shook hands with them. "We'll send the report over in about a week," I said, and headed toward the front door, with Mom and Dad following me as if they wanted to herd me out.

With my hand on the doorknob, I made one last stand. Turning to them, I focused on Dad and said, "I'm sorry if I crossed a line. It's just…well, you remind me so much of my own father. He and my mom moved into a condo a few years ago, and he just shriveled up and died there." I couldn't help it; my voice caught on the last bit. I cleared my throat. "Anyway, I've taken enough of your time. Nice meeting you both." And I walked out into the sunshine as they shut the door behind me.

When I reached the street, I turned and took one last look at our old house. I thought I could hear Mom and Dad arguing inside.

I turned back to the street with a hopeful smile, and saw the jetway steps right in front of me. After one more glance back at the house, I mounted the stairs.

The jetway took me back to the gate area. I glanced around for the old man in the boater, but he was nowhere to be seen. As I looked around for him, I heard the last call for my flight. I picked up my feet and made it onto the plane just before the flight attendant closed the door.

As I eased into my seat, my phone chirped. It was a text message from my sister: *Are you on the plane yet?*

Just boarded, I texted back.

Can't wait to see you! This is going to be the best birthday surprise for Dad ever!

I grinned to myself and texted, *Right? It'll be so good to be home.*

Revenge of the Remora

As I've said before, I try to stay away from the most overdone tropes in fantasy and horror. But I couldn't resist the chance to write a vampire story — not after I was handed the gift of the title by someone in the Books Untamed group on Facebook. This story is another plus-a-few — it appeared in Boo!: Volume II *in October 2014.*

This time, it was supposed to be different.

This time, I was to take the world by storm. I was to have my pick of nubile beauties, all drawn to me by my powerful, irresistible voice. That was why I formed this musical ensemble in the first place. Goth music — ha! These mindless dandies have no idea what real *Gothic music was like. It was tasteful. Restrained. It certainly didn't involve banging any heads. Or screaming.*

The screaming came later.

Alas, this is a coarser time. And alas for me, I still have a...taste...for beautiful women. But the ensemble draws only babies with bad makeup and frightful taste in clothing. And even to attract those, I had to recruit that...boy.

Now that the ensemble has achieved some fame, the boy has become insufferable. He plays the vamp outrageously. He needs must be managed. Yet fool that I am, I swore an oath that I would not slake my thirst amongst my fellow musicians.

No, I must have a proxy. And I have found one. I have taken pains to set the stage, as they say, and tonight, justice will be served....

"Are you coming?" Taffy's roommate Charli poked her head around the bedroom door. "Ooh, you look spectacular!"

Taffy smiled archly at her reflection in the mirror, and licked her teeth to remove the blood-red lipstick where it had smeared. "I know," she said, giving herself another once-over, from the top of her jet-black head to the tips of her jet-black boots. She had known that the miniskirt, studded and draped with chains, would be the perfect addition to her ensemble when she saw it at the mall earlier in the day – and she had been right. She glanced over at Charli and grinned. "You look amazing, too."

Charli grinned back and struck a pose, safety-pin earrings swaying gently as she shook out her hair. Her eyes danced as she relaxed into her usual slouchy stance. "Ryan's just got to notice us tonight."

"He will if he knows what's good for him," Taffy purred, and both young women erupted in giggles. Then Taffy reached for the tube of dental adhesive and the package of tiny, pointy eyetooth caps. "Let me just put my teeth on and we can go."

The two of them been anticipating this night for weeks – ever since Charli had heard that her high school friend Ryan was coming to town for a concert. Of course, he wasn't called Ryan anymore; now he was Raoul the Vile, front man for Ambush the Gates, the most popular Goth vampire band in the history of the planet. They weren't *real* vampires, of course; they only played them onstage – rising out of coffins and squirting fake blood into the audience as they shredded their top-selling songs.

But famous as he was, Raoul hadn't forgotten his roots. Charli had called his mom and, through her, talked him into giving them free tickets and backstage passes.

Charli chattered happily all the way into town on the subway, oblivious to the stares of the other riders. "Ryan was just another guy in high school, you know? I mean, we all had crushes on him because he played the guitar. But to think he's somebody famous now. And I *know* him! And we get to meet the band!" She squealed and grabbed Taffy's arm, then subsided with a happy sigh. "This night is a dream come true."

Taffy hugged her friend but said nothing. She couldn't. She had told Charli that she had a crush on Raoul, too, but what Charli didn't know, and what Taffy didn't plan to tell her, was that Taffy's was deeper – deeper and more true. She was sure she was the girl for him. It was fated. She had seen it in a dream. All she needed to do was get close to him, and then he would understand. He would pick her over Charli. And while she would feel sorry for Charli, she was sure another member of the band would want to date her. That way, they could still be friends.

The concert passed in a blur, helped along by the secondhand pot smoke wafting through the audience. At one point, Charli waved madly and yelled, "Ryan!" Raoul glanced their way and winked, sending Charli into a paroxysm of joy. But Taffy couldn't move. *He saw me. He saw me, and winked. It's all coming true.*

After the show, Charli pulled Taffy toward the burly security guard at the backstage entrance and flashed him their passes. The guy grabbed the passes, lifted his sunglasses to study them, and finally motioned toward the door. Charli bounced in place, squealing, and dashed through. Taffy followed, her heart in her throat.

"Hey, Charleen!" the famous voice called. Taffy turned as he stalked toward them, towering over them in his high-heeled boots. As he got closer, she could see the black powdered dye in his hair, and the lines of pale skin where he had sweated through his white pancake makeup.

Raoul swept Charli into an embrace. "It's so good to see you."

"Hey, Ryan," Charli said, disentangling herself for a moment. "Great concert! Thanks for the passes. Oh!" She reached for Taffy's hand and pulled her over. "This is my friend Taffy. Taffy, this is Ryan." She beamed.

"Hey, Taffy," said Raoul. "Nice to meet you."

"Nice to meet…" Taffy said, her voice trailing off. Raoul had already turned back to Charli, and Taffy couldn't help noticing that his hand had found her friend's butt. Dismay flooded through her, reddening her face until she was sure it showed through her own dead-white makeup.

"Hey, don't you ladies go anywhere," Ryan/Raoul was saying. "We're gonna party hearty tonight and you're invited." He flashed a grin in Taffy's direction as he hugged Charli closer. "Just let me go change and get this makeup off so I don't look like a freak in public, and we'll get out of here."

"Isn't he amazing?" Charli bubbled.

Taffy couldn't respond. All she could do was stare after him as his words echoed in her head: *Get this makeup off, so I don't look like a freak. Like a freak. A freak.*

This was turning into the worst night of her life.

From the shadows, I watch her dreams turn to dust. Her dismay is so strong I can almost taste it. Ah! It has been too long. My hunger demands satiation. But stay a moment longer – anticipation is delicious, too....

The girls rode to the party in a limo with Ryan and the rest of the band. All of the men had changed into jeans, and without their costumes and makeup, they looked like normal guys. Ryan sat between the two women on the forward-facing seat, with his arms draped across the back; the other three men sat across from them. Sid, the bass player, sat across from Taffy; he stared out the window in silence. Snake, the drummer, sat in the middle and wiggled his tongue sinuously at her every time she made the mistake of looking at him. Viscount Edouard, who played rhythm guitar and sang backup, regarded her with hooded eyes from the far corner of the car.

Snake was gross, she decided, but Edouard creeped her out. She felt herself shrinking into her own corner as drinks and a marijuana pipe made the rounds.

The party was at a private home, but Taffy never did meet the hosts. The proceedings were in full swing by the time they arrived. Charli and Ryan disappeared immediately. *No doubt they're already in a bedroom upstairs. How could I have been so stupid?* She tossed off a beer, and then another.

"Who's that?" she heard someone ask as she wandered the rooms with her third beer.

"Remora," someone else – Sid? – said dismissively. "She came with Raoul and some other girl."

"Ugh. Groupies," the first guy said, his voice dripping with disgust.

Is that what those guys think of us? She wanted to drop through the floor. No, she wanted to go home. But she had no idea how to get out of here, or even where they were.

Maybe if she got drunk enough, she could forget the conversation she had just overheard. She drained her red plastic cup in one long gulp, and went back toward the bar.

The bassist fancies himself too good for all of this. He is not, of course, but that is of no consequence. He is good enough for this musical project of mine. And all unwittingly, he has assisted my other project, too.

I am nearly dizzy with anticipation. Her heartbeat calls to me; I can almost feel her warm blood on my lips. At last, the denouement is at hand!

"Taffy!" she heard Charli call. Her friend whizzed past her in Ryan/Raoul's wake. "Come on! There's a pool in the backyard!" She grabbed Taffy's hand and pulled.

"I didn't bring my suit," Taffy protested, but Charli just laughed at her.

As soon as they got outside, Taffy could see why: everyone in the pool was naked. She couldn't help but stare as Ryan/Raoul stripped off his clothes and dove in, with Charli, laughing, right after him.

"Not going in?" a cultured voice at her elbow inquired. Startled, she turned to see Edouard standing a little too close. She was sure he hadn't been there a second ago.

To cover her confusion, she decided to try to make conversation – and immediately regretted it. "Are you really a viscount?" she blurted.

"I was," he said. "Once."

"Oh." She didn't know what else to say.

"I have been watching you," he continued, moving closer; she could feel his breath on her cheek. "This evening is not turning out the way you had hoped it would, is it?"

Tears stung her eyes. "No," she confessed. "Not at all."

"You want him, do you not?" Eduoard nodded toward Raoul.

"Yes," she said, wondering briefly why she was admitting her feelings to this creepy guy.

"And you hate her."

"I do," she said, surprising herself with her vehemence as she watched Charli frolicking naked with the man of her dreams. Raoul had been promised to her. It was fated. And Charli was getting in her way. Something needed to be done about that.

"I can help you," Edouard said, as if he had read her thoughts. Drawing her into the shadows, he said, "You can still have it all, my dear. You can have the revenge you seek." He nuzzled her neck for a moment. "Just leave everything to me."

A short time later, they emerged from the darkness. Taffy felt transformed, and wondered why she had ever thought of Edouard as creepy. He had given her a wondrous gift, and now she was going to share it with the man of her dreams.

She smiled gratefully at Edouard as she began to remove her clothing at the side of the pool. The chains on her miniskirt clattered as they hit the concrete deck. "Thank you," she said, feeling something loosen in her mouth as she spoke. She raised her dead-white hand to her mouth and spat the fake eyeteeth into her palm. Then she threw them into the grass. She didn't need them anymore; her new, real eyeteeth pricked her lower lip as she smiled.

"Oh, no, my dear," he said. "I must thank *you*. I have bided my time, awaiting the opportunity to seek my own revenge on Raoul. He thinks to play the vampire without a care for the cost. Now he will learn the fate of those who steal the spotlight from Edouard. Go, my dear. Go, and spread my gift."

As she slipped into the pool and swam toward Raoul with sure strokes, she could hear Edouard murmur, as clearly as if he still stood next to her, "Yes, go. Share my gift with Raoul. Then you and he shall be together for eternity."

"For eternity," she breathed as she slipped between Raoul and Charli, and fastened herself on his neck. His heartbeat, strong and steady, aroused her; she bit more deeply and drank.

She felt Raoul stiffen. Then his arms came around her as she bent him backwards toward the surface of the water.

"Taffy?" Her rival's voice came to her as if from very far away. "What are you doing? Hey, he's bleeding!" Taffy felt someone pounding on her back. "Get away from him, Taffy! Help! Someone help us! She's killing him!"

It was true, she realized dimly; his heartbeat was slowing and the froth of life in her mouth had slowed to a trickle. She let go, and he splashed into the pool, the water turning a faint pink near the twin puncture wounds on his neck.

And so I am undone.

I thought only to cow, not to kill. I should have known not to unleash one so young and untrained on so crucial an errand. Alas, it has been too long since I attempted such a plot. As always, my desire has swept me away....

My most profound apologies, my dear child. I release you.

"You crazy bitch!" Charli screamed. But as Taffy turned toward her rival, the woman's expression turned from hatred to fear.

"Oh, God," Taffy breathed. "I didn't mean to do that." She wiped her lips with the back of her hand, and looked at it, seeing the water droplets mix with blood. She shuddered. It felt as if she were awakening from a dream. "It wasn't supposed to be like this." She looked toward the shadowed corner where she knew Edouard still stood and whispered, "I'm sorry."

She heard him sigh with regret. "As am I, my dear. But it can't be helped now," he said. "Finish it. We must go before the police arrive."

She realized she and Charli were alone in the pool with Raoul's aimlessly drifting corpse; the others had fled. She was hyper-aware of sounds: screams and pounding feet in the house; the front door opening and slamming repeatedly; a siren wailing in the distance; and the blood pounding in Charli's veins.

Sweet, sweet blood. It sang to her.

"I'm sorry," she whispered again, as she wrapped her friend in an embrace, stilling her flailing arms, and sank her teeth into her neck.

What was it that Scottish poet said about the best-laid plans? Never mind. It has not all been for naught, for I have gained a child. And as for fame? Why, I have all eternity to try again.

The Only Way to Save You

I wrote this flash fiction piece for one of the weekly contests at Indies Unlimited, but it didn't win. I gave it a bit of a rewrite, and it ended up instead in 13 Bites Vol. I.

Captain Benedict halted us just below the ridgetop and waited for Morton, our scout, to return. The rest was welcome. We'd been crossing enemy territory since sunup, and everybody was on edge.

At length, Morton returned. I was too far away to hear what he said, but when he gestured toward the passage to our northwest, the captain pulled his sidearm and shot him in the head.

"Move out," was all Captain Benedict said.

As I passed the dead man sprawled in the dirt, I offered up a silent prayer. Morton had been my friend. He'd never been anything but loyal. What game was Benedict playing?

I watched the captain through narrowed eyes. As we approached the mouth of the northwest passage, he seemed to tip his hat. But to whom?

I scanned the landsacape. Then, on impulse, I looked up – just as the massive cube uncloaked. I shouted, but there was no escape; a column of light shot down, engulfing us.

My stomach lurched. A million angry insects seemed to be taking me apart, cell by cell.

A moment later, or maybe many thousands of moments later, the sensation passed. Our whole column – one hundred fifty men and women – had been transported from the pristine wilderness to an alien cargo bay.

As my fellow soldiers stumbled and retched, I forgot about rank. I marched up to Benedict and yelled, "Damn you! You've betrayed us to the enemy! Why? *Why?*"

Laughter bubbled from his lips. "Only way to save you," he wheezed.

"He's crazy," someone said.

"Not at all," said another voice, oily and alien. The vile creature approached, its tentacles slapping the floor. "He's become one of us. As will you.

"We will have this world. Your people must choose: assimilation or death. Your captain has already chosen for you."

The last thing I heard, before I was turned inside out, was Benedict's eerie laughter.

Like Selling Vacuum to a Dargonite

I like to read science fiction, *but I don't write it very well. Sci-fi fans are a tough crowd; I'm always convinced that any whizz-bang technology I might invent won't be whizz-bang enough to keep them happy. In this story, which appeared in* Plan 559 from Outer Space *in the spring of 2015, I hoped the humor would distract purists from the story's technological failings.*

Ottheimer Hoople III had gone into space determined to make a name for himself.

He already had a name, of course, and quite a famous one. Everyone knew the story of how his grandfather had founded the first vacuum-extraction facility on Dargos Nine. Before the original Ott Hoople had come along, nobody knew why they would even need a vacuum. After all, wasn't space full of it? It was, of course – but it took a genius of Ott's stature to figure out a way to package it in a household-size quantity without the sides of the container collapsing inwards, and then to write *99 Household Uses for Hoople's Canned Vacuum.* The book was an instant bestseller, and his fellow Dargonites lined up in virtual queues that stretched for virtual blocks in order to get their hands on a copy, complete with a sample can. This was, of course, the source of the popular phrase, *It's like selling vacuum to a Dargonite.*

That rankled Ott III's father, Ottheimer Hoople Jr. He considered the whole operation a shameful scam, and spoke openly about how it had made the Hoople name a laughingstock. The original Ott ignored Ott Jr. until he began to gather followers, at which point Granddad disowned his son, leaving Ott Jr. to a life of penury.

That rankled Ott III. Particularly the part about growing up poor. His father would go on and on about ethics and the high moral ground, but all Ott III knew was that his cousins were dining on rare roast bloon imported from the Acturax system, while he and his parents made do with chokeseed gruel.

As soon as he could, Ott III lied about his age – and his name – and hired on as crew of a trans-system freighter hauling cargoes of questionable legality for an unknown entity. Pretty soon, Ottmar Heap had sweet-talked his way into a spot on the bridge. Then into the captain's chair.

Then he did a little digging and discovered that his secretive employer was a methane breather from Zrthn whose only vice was gambling. Our hero arranged to meet the creature – purely by happenstance, of course – in a Doffin-sector gambling den. There, he challenged it to a game of dice. The methane breather never caught on to the fact that Ott was using loaded dice. It just kept playing, more and more frantically, until Ott had won not just his own ship, *Cassini's Purse*, but the creature's whole fleet – among them, a Reagan-class diplomatic cruiser called *Wisdom's Pride*.

Ott had never felt called to politics before. He had surmised early on that there were more straightforward ways to cheat people. But owning *Wisdom's Pride* made him rethink his earlier stance.

Well, that, and meeting her captain. Alessandra Poink had a wondrous body, and a mind as crafty as Ott's.

"It's gonna be a piece of cake, Ottie," Alix said as they lay entwined together in her bunk in the *Pride*'s luxurious captain's suite. "All we have to do is find a mark."

"But Alix, my sweet," said Ottie, nibbling her delectable earlobe, "I thought diplomatic cruisers couldn't be corrupted."

"They can't," she said with a wink. "Unless you know the right security codes." Then she did something to him, and something else, and all thoughts of marks and security codes fled from his mind for a time.

But it all came back to him later, as he sprawled in his own bunk aboard the far more spartan *Cassini's Purse*. He fed certain parameters into the shipboard computer and had it run a galaxy-wide search. In less than three minutes, he had his answer.

He pinged Alix on their own private channel. "I got the mark," he told her with a lazy grin.

"And I got the codes," she purred. "This will be as easy as selling vacuum to a Dargonite."

He hoped she didn't see him wince.

Three weeks later, the reprogramming of *Wisdom's Pride* was complete, and Ott's fleet set a course for Xanthan Gin – a backwater planet that was nevertheless one of the richest prizes in all the galaxy. For just under the planet's crust, its core was comprised entirely of molten polysaccharite – the thinnest, strongest, and most flexible metal ever discovered. Plus, when ground to powder, it made a terrific replacement for flour in gluten-free recipes.

All of the polysaccharite mines on Xanthan Gin were operated by a government-owned corporation. And the government controlled the exports with an iron fist, claiming that a polysaccharite free-for-all might very well drain the planet's core to the point that the crust would collapse, leading to the rather precipitous deaths of several billion XGinners. But rumor had it that the real reason was to jack up the price, allowing government bureaucrats to live in sweet luxury while the vast majority of XGinners scrabbled in the mines.

Ott understood penury. He empathized with the XGinners. But he had no interest in rescuing them from their repressive government. No, he wanted to *be* the government.

Some decades previously, all diplomatic relations had been turned over to computers, with each computerized diplomat required to operate within certain defined parameters. The idea was to take qualities like hate, belligerence, posturing, and outright lies out of diplomacy; computers, it was thought, would be able to speak to one another dispassionately, thereby reducing the chance of war. And in fact, the incidence of armed conflict did drop by something in the neighborhood of seventy percent. However, the new rules took much of the fun out of it.

And as Alix had said, there were creative ways around those rules.

Cautiously, Ott and Alix made diplomatic contact with the XGin government – which is to say that the reprogrammed computer aboard *Wisdom's Pride* hailed the XGin diplomatic computer, and the two exchanged pleasantries.

At last, *Wisdom's Pride* broached the subject of its visit. <u>We would like to offer a business proposal for your consideration</u>, it said.

<u>Oh?</u>

<u>Yes. We represent an entity that wishes to remain anonymous for now. This entity proposes to become the official trade representative on behalf of Xanthan Gin to all outside worlds.</u>

The XGin diplomatic computer was silent for a few moments – running scenarios, Ott supposed. Finally, it said, <u>Interesting. How would this work?</u>

<u>We would relieve you of the burden of negotiating tiresome trade deals with those worlds interested in purchasing your polysaccharite. You, in return, would agree to bump up the retail price by thirty percent, which we would then retain as our profit.</u>

<u>So our profit would be the same, under your scheme, as it is now?</u>

<u>That is correct.</u>

Again, the XGin computer fell silent. Ott's fingernails dug crescent-shaped creases in his palms as he waited. His nerves were not cut out for this.

At last, the XGin computer said, <u>We require the identity of the entity offering us this opportunity.</u>

<u>That is not possible,</u> *Wisdom's Folly* returned.

Another, longer, silence. Ott thought he might have to scream to relieve his tension.

And then finally! <u>Transmit the programming to us so that we may append our agreement.</u>

<u>Transmitting now,</u> said *Wisdom's Folly*. <u>It has been a pleasure doing business with you.</u>

<u>And you</u>, the XGin computer returned politely. And seconds later, XGin sent back the approved contract. The deal was sealed.

That night, lolling in Alix's bed aboard *Wisdom's Folly*, the co-conspirators toasted their good fortune. "The most brilliant part of this," said Ottie, "is that the XGin computer believes it cannot be set up. It's forced to operate from a position of trust. It has to believe that we're honest." He cackled.

"And that's what's gonna make it so easy to screw 'em," Alix said.

"I'd like to screw you," he said, rolling over on top of her.

But she pushed him back flat. "Oh no, Ottie baby," she said as she clambered atop him. "I'm the one who's gonna screw *you*."

They let the operation run for a month. Then they sent their first bill to XGin.

A nanosecond later, the XGin diplomat contacted *Wisdom's Folly*. We believe there has been a misunderstanding, XGin said.

Oh?

Yes. There appear to be some charges on your invoice that we did not agree to.

We are very sorry to hear that, *Wisdom's Folly* said. We would be happy to clarify our invoice for you.

It is not clarification that is needed, said XGin. There are a number of line items on this invoice that we never agreed to. We would like them removed.

Such as?

Such as this line item for office supplies.

Surely you would agree that we are due compensation for our costs of doing business, *Wisdom's Folly* said reasonably.

Yes, but we assumed those costs would be rolled into your thirty percent markup.

Ah. You see? It is a misunderstanding, after all. Unfortunately, we are unable to include those costs as you suggest. They must be broken out just as we have listed them on our invoice.

And what of this line item for travel? What sort of travel arrangements would amount to thirty percent of the total price of the polysaccharite you brokered for us last month?

Surely you would not want us to look destitute when we travel on your behalf. Your buyers might begin to question whether XGin's operation is first class.

Yes, but…. XGin fell silent again for a moment. I suppose you will say the same of your entertainment expenses.

Of course. We are pleased that you agree.

We most certainly do not agree, XGin retorted. We would never have agreed to such usury as this. You are leaving us with only twenty-five percent of the profit from the sale of our polysaccharite last month.

That is so.

And if we break the contract, XGin said, sounding a tiny bit desperate, you are entitled to take ownership of our mining operations.

That is so.

We cannot live like this! This is extortion!

We are very sorry to hear you say this. Alas, we cannot offer you any discounts not previously negotiated. Our invoice is due and payable within fifteen days. And *Wisdom's Folly* cut its transmission.

Ott rubbed his hands together in glee. The trap was set. It only needed to be sprung.

Fifteen days later, it was. When XGin failed to pay the disputed invoice, Ott sent his fighters into the planet's atmosphere. XGin's defense system was good, but Ott's forces were better. In less than a day, he had taken control of the government.

The following day, he ordered the market price for polysaccharite frozen at the thirty-percent-higher rate.

On day three, he and Alix moved into the emperor's palace.

"This is the life," Ottie said, as he and Alix reclined in bed in their posh new digs. "A jug of wine, a loaf of the best gluten-free bread in the galaxy, and you beside me." He threw his arms wide. "What could go wrong?"

He heard a ruckus in the hallway, and looked a question at Alix. "He could," she said, hooking her thumb at the door.

As if on cue, the methane breather strode through the door.

"What...what are *you* doing here?" Ott spluttered.

The creature took a whiff from its inhaler and breathed out, "What are *you* doing in bed with *my wife?*"

"What?"

Alix cocked her head and smirked at him. "Sorry, Ottie. You didn't really think Hgtht would let you get away with his fleet that easily, did you?"

The fact that she could pronounce the creature's name told him it was all true. "But that...but you...?" he stammered. "And then you and I.... Augh!" He thought he might throw up.

Alix crossed to Hgtht and wrapped her arms around his ample middle. The creature took another big whiff of methane and said, "This is a proud day for Zrthn. I have my fleet back, and I now own the galaxy's biggest deposit of polysaccharite." He took another whiff. "But best of all, I have managed to trick a descendent of Ottheimer Hoople!"

Ott shrunk into his seat. "You knew who I was all along," he said miserably.

Alix threw back her head and laughed. "You made it too easy, Ottie," she said. "It was like selling vacuum to a Dargonite!"

About the Author

Lynne Cantwell writes mostly urban fantasy and paranormal romance, with a dash of magic realism when she's feeling more serious. She is also a contributing author for Indies Unlimited. In a previous life, she was a broadcast journalist who worked at Mutual/NBC Radio News, CNN, and a bunch of other places you have probably never heard of. She has a master's degree in fiction writing from Johns Hopkins University. Currently, she lives near Washington, D.C.

Other books by Lynne Cantwell:

The Pipe Woman Chronicles Universe

Seized: Book One of the Pipe Woman Chronicles
Fissured: Book Two of the Pipe Woman Chronicles
Tapped: Book Three of the Pipe Woman Chronicles
Gravid: Book Four of the Pipe Woman Chronicles
Annealed: Book Five of the Pipe Woman Chronicles
The Pipe Woman Chronicles Omnibus

Where Were You When: A Land, Sea, Sky Anthology
Crosswind: Land, Sea, Sky Book 1
Undertow: Land, Sea, Sky Book 2
Scorched Earth: Land, Sea, Sky Book 3
The Land Sea Sky Trilogy

Dragon's Web: Book One of the Pipe Woman's Legacy
Firebird's Snare: Book Two of the Pipe Woman's Legacy
Spider's Lifeline: Book Three of the Pipe Woman's Legacy
Turtle's Weir: Book Four of the Pipe Woman's Legacy

A Billion Gods and Goddesses: The Mythology Behind *The Pipe Woman Chronicles*

Stand-Alone Novels
SwanSong
The Maidens' War
Seasons of the Fool

Contributor
Indies Unlimited 2012 Flash Fiction Anthology
Indies Unlimited 2013 Flash Fiction Anthology
Indies Unlimited 2014 Flash Fiction Anthology
Indies Unlimited Tutorials and Tools for Prospering in a Digital World
Indies Unlimited Tutorials and Tools for Prospering in a Digital World, Vol. II
BookGoodies How to Write A Book
First Chapters
13 Bites
Summer Dreams
Boo!: Volume 2
Winter Tales
Plan 559 from Outer Space
Other Realms
13 Bites Vol. III
I Heard It on the Radio
Plan 559 from Outer Space Mk. II

Find Lynne on Teh Intarwebz:

Facebook: http://www.facebook.com/pages/Lynne-Cantwell
Twitter: http://twitter.com/lynnecantwell
Google Plus: http://plus.google.com/+LynneCantwell
Goodreads:
http://www.goodreads.com/author/show/696603.Lynne_Cantwell
Blog: http://www.hearth-myth.com